Praise for Connie Shelton

"Shelton continues to combine suspenseful storytelling
with sensitive portrayals of complex
family relationships." —*Booklist*

"...a wonderful, easy flow that draws in the reader."
—Amazon 5-Star review

"As for me, I enjoy mysteries infused with a little touch
of magic and a dream that anything is possible."
—Amazon 5-Star review

"For some thrills and high-rising suspense, and a clever
plot, this is one tale that cleverly spins …
with an ending that will blow you away."
-- *Coffee Time Romance*

"HIGHLY RECOMMENDED." -- *I Love a Mystery*

"Fighting off the bad guys with her usual panache,
Charlie once again proves she's one tough bird."
– *Booklist*

"There's a lot of action in this exciting thriller and
Connie Shelton gets better with every book she writes."
-- *The Midwest Book Review*

SWEET
HOLIDAYS

The Third Samantha Sweet Mystery

Connie Shelton

Secret Staircase Books

Sweet Holidays
Published by Secret Staircase Books, an imprint of
Columbine Publishing Group
PO Box 416, Angel Fire, NM 87710

This book is a work of fiction. Names, characters, places and
incidents are either the product of the author's imagination or are
used fictitiously. Any resemblance to actual events or locales or
persons, living or dead, is entirely coincidental.

Book layout and design by Secret Staircase Books
Cover illustration © Robisklp
Cover cupcake design © Basheeradesigns

Publisher's Cataloging-in-Publication Data

Shelton, Connie
Sweet Holidays / by Connie Shelton.
p. cm.
ISBN 978-1945422188 (paperback)

1. Samantha Sweet (Fictitious character)--Fiction. 2. Taos, New
Mexico—Fiction. 3. Paranormal artifacts—Fiction. 4. Bakery—
Fiction. 5. Women sleuths—Fiction. 6. Christmas stories. I. Title

Samantha Sweet Mystery Series : Book 3.
Shelton, Connie, Samantha Sweet mysteries.

BISAC : FICTION / Mystery & Detective / Cozy.

813/.54

*For Dan, the most wonderful partner
a writer could ask for.*

My eternal thanks to my excellent editor,
Susan Slater, for your insightful suggestions and for
all the good catches you make in reading my work.

And to my readers, my thanks for your loyalty and
for recommending my books to others; you make it all
worthwhile. You are the best!

Chapter 1

Samantha Sweet tucked a sprig of sugar holly against the Yule log cake she'd just created, her final one for the day. She tapped a sprinkling of powdered sugar over the chocolate rolled confection and called out to the front room. "Jennifer, this is ready for the display case."

Her petite assistant walked into the kitchen, dusting cookie crumbs from her purple apron with the Sweet's Sweets logo embroidered on it. The shop slogan, "A Bakery of Magical Delights" seemed especially appropriate this time of year. Sam always marveled at how Jen's makeup and dark hair in its neat chignon seemed nearly as fresh in the late afternoon as first thing in the morning.

"It's snowing out there," Jen commented, sending a smile toward the holiday pastry as she lifted it from Sam's work table.

"Think it will stick?"

Jen shrugged. "Hard to say. Probably not."

Sam washed her hands at the sink and followed Jen out to the sales area, pleased to see that the usual late afternoon customers had not let her down, despite the looming weather front. The first week of December was a little early for lasting snow, but the mountains of northern New Mexico could expect just about any weather this time of year. She walked over to the front windows of her shop and peered out into the deepening dusk. White pellets blew horizontally across the parking lot, gathering in small drifts against the curb.

"I can close up if you want to leave early," Sam told Jen. "I have to take a quick inventory and order more supplies anyway. That order for the county employees Christmas party wiped out a few of our necessities."

The younger woman looked up from the bistro tables where she'd been giving everything a quick wipe. She tucked a single strand of dark hair behind her ear and rinsed out her cleaning rag. "You sure? It's been a busy day for you, too."

"Luckily." Sam turned from the window. "I thought we'd have a big slowdown after all the Thanksgiving pies were gone, but it just hasn't happened. It's like everyone's on a sugar binge."

Jen wiggled her eyebrows. "And you're loving it!"

Sam felt her smile widen. "You bet!"

"I know we've talked about this before . . . A few customers have asked about candies. You know, chocolates, truffles and stuff like that."

Sam bit her lip. She'd definitely considered adding candy to the normal bakery offerings, but other than the cocoa she used in flavoring her frostings and decorations, she didn't have much experience with chocolate—only enough to know that it could really get tricky if it weren't tempered and handled correctly.

"I need to think about it, Jen. I can't afford to risk the reputation of the shop by putting out anything that isn't top quality. And I sure don't have the time this season to take classes and learn how to do it. Maybe later."

"Sure. Just passing along customer requests."

"I know. Thanks." Sam smiled as she glanced out the window again. "Go on now. And be careful—the visibility sucks."

Jen pulled off her apron and hung it on one of the hooks inside the work area. Sam locked the front door behind her, turned over the Closed sign, and dimmed the lights to their nighttime settings. Pulling the cash from the register, she carried it to the small desk she'd set up for herself in the back room and began counting. But her mind zipped in a hundred directions, and she found herself going back for a third count before she gave up and pulled out her calculator.

She liked the idea of adding candy to their offerings. Plus, they'd had several requests for Jewish holiday treats as well. Hanukkah would begin only four days before Christmas this year, so she really needed to address both holidays at once. Taos didn't have many Jews so Sam was only now learning about those traditional foods, let alone how to make them. Luckily, she thought her friend Zoë might have some of the recipes, and Sam planned on begging for help from that quarter. And, she'd already gotten orders for two Christmas themed weddings and another on New Year's Eve—cakes, table favors, and even some rather randy bachelorette treats.

Then there was her other job. Sam broke into houses—
legally, for the US Department of Agriculture—her main
source of steady income before the bakery came into
being. Now that finances were more stable and she had
a little nest egg, she could easily afford to quit that one,
but there was the little matter of her government contract.
Her supervising officer, Delbert Crow, didn't seem inclined
to simply let her out of it. For the moment, she'd had a
short breather. Lawns and shrubs took the winter off, thank
goodness, leaving Sam with only two properties where she
had to stop in for a few minutes a week, just to be sure no
pipes had frozen or roofs had leaked. So far, so good on
that count.

Her cell phone startled her out of that train of thought.
She pulled it from the pocket of her slacks.

"Mom?" Kelly's voice held a note of urgency.

"Yeah, hon?"

"I need a ride home. I'm at Romero's Garage."

"Problem with your car?"

"Kind of." Kelly stalled, in the same way Sam
remembered from her daughter's teen years. "Well, it's got
a bent wheel rim."

Sam bit the inside of her cheek, forcing herself not to
ask.

"Okay, okay. I went off the road."

Kelly's years of living in southern California hadn't
exactly prepared her for winters back here in the mountains.
"I'm just leaving the bakery. I should be there in ten or
fifteen minutes." Normally a trip to the garage that had
serviced her vehicles for years would take five minutes, but
tonight she had a feeling the streets were getting messy.

She stuffed her bank deposit into a zippered bag, gathered her coat and backpack, and rechecked the doors and lights before walking out into the alley behind the bakery. Her delivery van, with its elaborate design that looked like an overflowing box of baked treats, now sported a light powdered-sugar coating, and a skiff of white coated the ground. She scuffed the toe of her sneaker across the pavement to test the slickness of it. Not that bad. Kelly had probably just panicked. Unless she was texting. Sam sighed and muttered all the choice words she wanted to say to her daughter but probably wouldn't. There's only so much lecturing a mom can do after the kid hits thirty.

She unlocked the van and tossed her backpack inside, her thoughts darting from her daughter's predicament, to the supply order she'd not had time to place, to the ever-nagging question of what she could make for a quick dinner. She'd only begun to edge one hip toward the driver's seat when a man stepped out of the shadows.

Sam's heart thudded.

"Madam of the sweet shop? Please—do not leave."

His accent was European, something with hints of French and German, but not quite. She let the van's door stay between herself and the large man who walked slowly toward her. His clothing was rough—a heavy wool coat of dark brown or black, dusted with snowflakes, dark pants, thick boots, a soft wool hat. The six-foot frame and heavy facial features belied the delicate hands that reached toward her, palms upward.

Sam started to make an excuse for not digging into her wallet for some cash, but he interrupted.

"Please, Madam, I am here to helping you."

"Look, I'm really—"

He removed the hat, revealing dark hair that fluffed away from his scalp in thin wisps. "I am Gustav Bobul."

And I'm supposed to know you?

"Chocolatier extraordinaire."

She felt her eyebrows draw together in puzzlement.

"I create such lovely confections . . . the exquisite tastes to delight one's vision and one's palate. You need me."

Had Jen set this up?

"I'm not really looking to hire anyone right now. The holidays . . . we're very busy."

"I know this. Is no need to pay. I come to answer a great need for you."

How did he know?

"I'm really in a hurry right now, Mr—"

"Bobul. You simply call me Bobul."

"Yeah, well. I have to—"

"I understanding. I come back tomorrow." He did a little flourish with the hat, plopped it back onto his head, and walked up the alley. In under ten seconds he had disappeared into the storm.

Sam stared at the end of the alley, where sleet raced through the cone of light from a streetlamp. Only the sound of the wind greeted her.

Chapter 2

Kelly was waiting under the tiny awning in front of Romero's Garage, hunched into her thin, inadequate coat, staring toward the street when Sam pulled up.

"I'm so sorry, Mom. It happened so fast. I didn't even feel the car going out of control." The words tumbled out before Kelly had even closed her door.

The encounter with the mysterious stranger, Bobul— and watching out for crazy drivers on the road—had so occupied Sam's thoughts that she'd not prepared a lecture.

"Danny Romero says they can have the rim replaced sometime tomorrow."

Kelly fluffed the snow out of her brown curls and chattered on, something about getting parts from a dealership, but Sam's mind was elsewhere. Maybe she could

meet with the chocolatier—if he really showed up again—
and see what he had to offer. She would check with Jen;
perhaps her assistant really had sent him over.

Putting that subject on the back burner, she began a
mental inventory of what she had at home for a quick dinner.
With the early darkness and the fact that she'd stayed late at
the shop, she couldn't seem to summon up the energy for
a made-from-scratch meal or for a trip out of the way to
grab fast food. The little van seemed determined to take the
shortest way home and Sam merely followed along.

Shallow drifts coated the long driveway beside Sam's
house. The van gave a little sideways shudder when she
made the turn, but she straightened it and kept a steady pace
to her normal spot near the kitchen door. Her cell phone
rang before she'd shut off the ignition.

Delbert Crow, her contracting officer for her USDA
job, rattled out a bunch of data about a new property and
Sam missed most of it.

"Hang on just a second, Delbert. I'm not even in the
house yet. Let me get inside and take a few notes so I can
get out to the place tomorrow."

"No deal. I need you to check this one tonight."

She groaned. Kelly glanced in Sam's direction and
nodded toward the house. She got out and headed toward
the back door while Sam tried to concentrate on what
Delbert was saying.

"It's not officially in foreclosure yet. Mortgage is only
ninety days in arrears," he said. "But it's a valuable property
and we don't want frozen pipes and water damage."

Sam stared out at the whipping snow. The temperature
didn't seem that low.

As if he could read her mind, Delbert said, "Forecast is for the snow to move out within the next couple of hours and the temps to drop. A lot. Just give it a quick check and make sure the heat is on. If the guy is as delinquent in his gas and electric as he is with the mortgage, everything could be shut down."

So much for getting off her feet and spending a snug evening at home. She clicked off the call and grabbed her backpack.

In the kitchen, Kelly was standing in front of the open refrigerator door, staring.

"Find whatever you want," Sam said. "I think there's some canned soup, or there might be homemade chile in the freezer if you want to take the time to thaw it. Delbert informs me that I have a must-do job tonight."

Kelly sent a sympathetic look. "I could make something and have it ready for when you get back."

"That's okay. I don't know how long it will take. You go ahead. I'll grab something when I get back."

One thing about breaking into houses—you never really knew what you were in for until you got there.

Sam slipped out of her heavy coat and went into her bedroom to change into something more suitable than her lightweight work slacks and baker's jacket. She took off her favorite gold earrings and put them into the odd, lumpy wood box that had come into her possession a few months earlier. As usual, the wood began to glow with warmth when she handled it. She quickly set it back on her dresser.

Ten minutes later, attired in sweats and sturdy boots, with a moisture proof jacket, she walked out to her big red Silverado 4X4 and let it warm up while she swept the coating of sleet off the windshield. Residual energy from handling the mysterious box ran through her but Sam really just wanted to get Delbert's chore over with. She put the truck in four-wheel mode and headed out.

She turned right at the end of her lane, away from the center of town and the plaza, where there were likely to be more traffic problems. A few more jogs along back roads and she'd bypassed most of the congested areas.

By the time she reached the south end of town and the tiny community of Talpa, she felt as if she were alone on the road. Tire tracks in the few inches of snow indicated where people had come home and turned at their driveways. Soft golden light, diffused by the whiteness in the air, glowed from most of the windows.

Darn it, that's where I want to be, she grumbled to herself. She gunned the truck just a little and came to the final turn, a narrow lane with only a few houses. She spotted her goal, a walled property that she guessed to be two or three acres, thickly treed behind the house. Sam stopped next to a heavy wooden gate in the adobe wall, which closed off the driveway. She grabbed her flashlight from under the seat.

An oversized wooden mailbox stood by a smaller walk-through gate and a peek inside showed that no one had picked up mail in ages. Sam closed the door on it and re-fastened the little hook that kept it in place. She put her shoulder to the gate and shoved, managing to get it open enough to squeeze through. Her latest diet clearly wasn't accomplishing quite as much as she'd hoped.

She looked toward the house, a large adobe with territorial style porch and pitched metal roof. A lawn stretched in a smooth unbroken expanse, and winding flowerbeds held snowy clumps of dead stalks that had never been trimmed back at the end of the summer. Neatly trimmed junipers, coated now with ice, flanked both sides of the front entry. Sam let out a frosty breath and started up the flagstone walk, watching her balance.

The front door appeared to be firmly locked. No surprise there. It was an expensive lock. In fact, an expensive door—carved wood with a little window inset near the top with a rustic iron grid over it. Tied to one of the small iron bars was a flame-red tag. Sam recognized it as the type normally left to inform the owner that the electric company planned to cut the power for non-payment. Sam held the tag up, and shined the flashlight's beam at it. The penned-in date for cut-off was the next day.

From her coat pocket she pulled her cell phone and speed-dialed Delbert Crow's number. He grumbled when she explained the situation and asked whether his department could make a plea to keep the power on.

"Doubt they'll do it," he said. "You better shut off the water line."

Life would be so much easier if people just handled their business. Every one of these houses had a different situation, and Sam wasn't even sure whether this place had a hookup to the city water main. She trudged around the side of the house, aiming the light beam about, until she came to a small outbuilding that apparently housed the well and pump. At least this was something with which she'd had experience. She quickly located the shutoff valve and heard the water settle into the tank. If there truly were a hard freeze before she could get power back to the place, there might still be damage. And that would end up becoming the problem of some insurance company.

Sam completed her circle of the house, not finding a single open door or window to ease the task of getting inside. A trip back to the truck would provide the tools to drill the lock, but she belatedly remembered that she didn't have a spare lockset and it wouldn't be smart to leave the place unsecured. She faced the solid front door again, stomping snow from her boots as she debated what to do.

On the off chance that the owner had left a hidden key, Sam ran her hand along the top of the door frame. Nothing. Large potted evergreens stood at each end of the covered porch but a thorough inspection of the pots, the drainage dishes they sat upon, and the earth around the plants yielded nothing. There wasn't a whole lot more she could do at this point, with all the hardware stores closed. She took a peek at her watch and saw that it was nearly ten. And she had to be up by five to open the bakery. It had been a long day. She gave the heavy door one more tug and turned back toward her truck.

The icy pellets stopped flying before she got home and when she stepped out of the truck she caught a glimpse of a few stars in the black sky. She would definitely need to get anti-freeze into the drains at the Talpa house tomorrow.

She kicked snow off her boots and opened the connecting door from the service porch to the kitchen, realizing belatedly that lights blazed in every room.

"Kelly? What's up?" Sam called out.

Her daughter appeared from the living room, wearing a pair of men's pajama bottoms and a fuzzy top, along with vivid purple furry socks. Her face was suffused with red and her eyes looked unnaturally bright.

"Kel?"

Her fingers twisted at the waist cord on the pajamas and her voice came out high and wavery. "Oh, Mom, I'm so worried. Beau called. They think Iris had a stroke."

Chapter 3

Sheriff Beau Cardwell's elderly mother was already wheelchair-bound with arthritis and severe osteoporosis. This couldn't be good. A wave of heat coursed through Sam—a hot flash, or simply the layers of winter clothing? She ripped at the zipper on her coat and slipped it off her shoulders, struggling to find her cell phone somewhere down deep in a pocket. She saw that she'd missed two calls.

"What else did Beau say?"

"They took her to the hospital. It must have been right after I left their house," Kelly fretted. She'd worked for the Cardwells ever since Sam began dating Beau, and they'd both developed strong affection for the older woman.

"Is she——?"

"I don't know. He said the doctors were still in there

with Iris when he called. It was maybe an hour ago?"

Sam was already punching the speed dial number for Beau's cell. No answer. It went immediately to voice mail. She snapped her phone shut and set it on the counter while she pulled off another layer of too-warm clothing.

"What happens with a stroke, Mom? Will she come home right away?"

"I don't think there's any way to know yet, hon." Sam glanced at the clock. It was way past their normal bedtimes, but she knew neither of them would get any sleep at this point. "Want some tea?"

Kelly nodded blankly.

"Here, Kel. Untangle your fingers from that pajama cord and sit down." Sam steered her daughter toward the kitchen table. "I'll try calling Beau again in a minute."

She turned a burner on under the tea kettle and reached for the canister of tea bags on the counter.

"I don't want anything to happen to Iris," Kelly said, sniffling into a tissue that Sam had handed her.

"I know, hon."

"She's such a sweetie. I mean, she's kind of like a better grandma."

Sam gave her daughter a sideways look.

"Well, you know what I mean. Since we never spent that much time around Gramma and Grampa . . ."

Sam patted Kelly's shoulder before she was interrupted by the whistling kettle on the stove. She knew exactly what Kelly meant. Beau's mother was one of those spirited old women with a sunny outlook on life and a keen sense of humor. Her own mother tended to be sharp-edged, with a "things are done a certain way" attitude. It was one reason Sam had gotten out of her small Texas hometown the minute she graduated from high school and had never looked back.

She picked up the two mugs of tea and headed for the kitchen table at the same moment her cell phone began to vibrate on the countertop.

"Here," she said, stretching toward Kelly with one of the mugs. "It's Beau."

Grabbing up the phone, she answered with, "Beau, I'm here."

"Hey, darlin'. Sorry I missed you earlier. Did Kelly tell you what—"

"Yes. How is she?"

"Mama's hanging in there."

That wasn't exactly a positive report.

"They have her sedated for the night and I need to go home and see to the dogs. I'm only about a block from your house."

"Come on over. Well, if you can spare the time."

He clicked off with a promise to stop by, and she heard the engine of his blue Explorer in the driveway less than three minutes later.

She watched him step out of the SUV and tug the collar of his sheepskin jacket tighter around his neck. Tiny flakes were coming down in fitful little slivers, a fraction of the earlier blizzard. He greeted her at the service porch, with a quick kiss and a frosted arm around her shoulders. His eyes looked tired, his normally ready smile a bit on the wan side.

"Hi, Kelly," he said, as he entered the kitchen after stomping his boots.

Sam held up the second mug of tea to him but he shook his head.

"I better not stay. Need to get feed out for the horses and dogs and then get back to the hospital."

"What are the doctors saying?" Kelly abandoned her own cup and walked toward Beau.

"Mama could go just about any direction at this point," he said. "She's got some loss of motion on her left side, and we haven't been able to get her to talk yet. But they say that's not uncommon. Aside from the problems that keep her in the wheelchair, she's a pretty healthy old bird. Strong heart and lungs . . . we'll just have to see how much everything else is affected."

Kelly's eyes welled up again.

"Hey, as Mama would say if she were sitting here, don't borrow trouble. I was with her when it happened and we got her to the hospital right away. Now we can only wait and see what happens. A lot of stroke victims recover really well."

Kelly nodded. Sam watched her expression brighten, but she wasn't so sure how well a woman in her eighties would rebound. She kept her silence.

"Well," said Beau, "I just wanted to stop by."

"If there's anything we can do . . ." Sam knew the words sounded hollow. It was something everyone said, but in reality what could they actually do? "Let us know when she can have visitors."

"She'll be in the hospital several days, minimum, and then a rehab facility." He didn't say so but Sam knew from his expression that Iris was nowhere near safe yet.

He shuffled a little, then gave Kelly a quick hug. Sam

walked him to the back door and pulled him into her arms. His kiss was grateful. She watched him drive down the snowy lane.

"I should have offered to go out there and take care of the animals myself," Kelly said when Sam walked back inside.

Sam gave her a look. Kelly, the girl who'd spent the past ten years living in L.A., miles from the nearest horse, the girl who'd never really gone through that horse-loving period that so many pre-teen girls did.

"And how——?"

"I've watched what Beau does, Mom. I could chop the ice off the water trough and scoop oats for them. He keeps some kind of a big bin of feed out in the barn."

"Sorry. I didn't mean to belittle your efforts. It would be a very nice thing to do. Why don't you call him back and offer to start tomorrow?"

Sam half listened to their conversation while she tidied the kitchen and headed toward her room to change into her nightshirt.

"He says he's got it covered," Kelly said, peeking in at Sam's bedroom door. She gave a small, dejected shrug.

In her concern for Iris, Sam hadn't even thought about how the loss of her job would impact Kelly. When her daughter had shown up in September, jobless and homeless, the paycheck for becoming Iris's caregiver was her lifeline to getting caught up on some bills she'd accumulated. But Sam worried that Beau couldn't afford to pay his mother's medical expenses and continue Kelly's salary, even with his promotion from deputy to sheriff last month.

All those thoughts continued to ramble through Sam's

head while she brushed her teeth and said goodnight to Kelly. Alone in her room, she wondered how Iris's condition would impact the budding romance between Beau and herself as well. They'd seen quite a lot of each other in September and early October. Then she opened her pastry shop and Beau's boss, the former sheriff, had gotten himself entangled in a scandal. Sam knew she had to take more than half the blame for the waning relationship but she really hated to see any distance develop between them.

Then she felt guilty for even having those thoughts while poor Iris might be lying in the hospital, permanently incapacitated or even dying.

She crawled into bed and pulled the thick comforter up to her chin, willing back the tears that threatened. Exhaustion overtook her the minute she turned out the light and she feel into a solid sleep.

An icy chill spread through the room, seeping even through the quilts and comforter on Sam's bed. She rolled over and saw that the red numerals on her clock showed 4:27. As tempting as it felt to try to burrow further in, she knew the alarm would go off in another three minutes. She reached a wary arm out and patted the empty side of the bed where she'd left her fleece robe. How had the room gotten so cold?

Even her Uggs felt chilly as she slipped her feet into them. Out in the hall, she could hear Kelly milling around. She switched on a lamp and slapped at the top of her clock as the alarm began to sound, fumbled her arms into the sleeves of her robe and headed for the bedroom door.

"Is the whole house this cold?" Kelly asked as Sam emerged. "My room is freezing."

"I better check the heater. Something's not right." Sure enough, a hand against the hallway register revealed only cold metal.

"Try lighting a burner on the stove," Sam told Kelly. "See if we've got gas."

A minute later: "It works. I'll put water on for tea."

Sam bundled back into her sweats and work boots and fetched her warm coat from the hook near the back door. They had electricity and gas, so something was wrong with the heater itself. Stepping out into the pre-dawn yard she glanced up to see a clear black sky and a million stars. Drawing a deep breath she could tell that the temperature, as predicted, had dropped. With a flashlight in hand, she made her way to the hatch that led to the crawl space under the house. What a pain. She'd debated for years about having a trapdoor installed inside, but the extra expense never seemed worth it.

Ten minutes later, she'd relit the blown-out pilot light and waited for the reassuring whoof as the heater kicked on and the blower began to distribute warm air to the ducts. She clumped back inside and found Kelly huddled at the kitchen table. Having decided that tea wasn't going to charge her batteries this morning, she'd started a pot of coffee and was staring at the carafe wistfully.

"Give the heater thirty minutes or so and we should be toasty warm again," Sam said.

Kelly sent a thankful grin her way.

Sam rushed through a quick shower, letting the hot water run hard enough to fill the room with steam. A relief from the chill air, but not quite enough to make the tile underfoot bearable. She dressed in her standard black slacks and baker's jacket and fluffed her short hair for a couple of minutes with the dryer. A swipe of lipstick and she was ready to walk out the door.

"Becky called while you were in the shower," Kelly said. "It's a two-hour delay for school."

Sam grumbled a little but that was the agreement with her assistant baker—the young mother of two had to be home when her kids weren't in school.

"She said she'd come in around ten." Still in her robe, with a biscuit and second cup of coffee in front of her, Kelly was making the most of her car-less state. She'd told Sam last night that a friend could take her by the garage to pick it up as soon as Joey Romero called to say that it was ready.

"No new word about Iris this morning?" Sam asked.

"It's only five, Mom. Even Beau probably wouldn't call this early."

Unless it were dire news. Neither of them said it.

Sam started her pickup truck and let it warm up while she went to the garage for a gallon of the special RV antifreeze she used for indoor plumbing. She would need to get out to that house in Talpa soon since the co-op planned to shut off the power today.

Her headlights cut a swath of light down her dark, abandoned lane. No one wanted to be out before daylight on a morning like this. Traffic had beaten down most of the snow but there were icy patches, formed by last night's sleet and wind. Her four-wheel-drive handled it fairly well but she was happy to arrive safely at the bakery ten minutes later.

Firing up the large commercial bake oven, she started the morning routine that had become second nature . She stirred up batters for her special blueberry and caramel-apple muffins and while they baked she set the mixer to blend the buttery dough for crumb cake. By the time Jennifer arrived to open the front door, Sam had racks of goodies ready to go and the scent of cinnamon and cloves filled the air.

"Good morning!" Jen greeted. "I can't believe how I never get tired of walking in here and taking a deep breath."

The two women lifted racks of still-warm muffins and headed to the sales room.

"Who's that?" Jen asked, nodding toward the front windows.

Sam glanced up from placing muffins into the display case. Staring into the bakery was a giant of a man wearing a pristine white baker's jacket and tall paper cap. Bobul had returned.

Chapter 4

He pecked at the window with a fingernail when Sam didn't immediately move to let him in. She sighed and set down her tray. He bustled in the moment she opened the door, the heavy brown coat draped over his arm.

"Mr. Bobul," she began, "we didn't really have—"

"Is no problem," he said, glancing around the bakery, taking in the bistro tables and chairs, the window displays with their holiday themed cakes, the vintage wooden cases that would soon be filled with breakfast pastries. "Bobul will find small space to work."

He turned to Jen and gave a formal little bow. "Gustav Bobul, master chocolatier, at your service."

She glanced at Sam, then back at the large man with the delicate hands.

He patted the side of a canvas messenger bag with a large strap that crossed his chest. "I bring my tools. Kitchen is——?" He glanced toward the doorway that led to the work area. Without waiting for Sam's response, he headed that direction.

"But we really didn't——" She bustled after him.

She caught up with him in the kitchen, where he was running his hands over the surface of the stainless steel work table. Before she could utter a word, he'd plopped his floppy bag on the table and pulled out a heavy bag of cocoa beans, some plastic molds and several small packets.

"Bobul——"

"Is no problem about the money, Miss Samantha. Remember, I say I will work for no pay." He turned back to the items on the table before she could respond.

The timer on her crumb cake went off just then and Sam hurried to the oven to check it. Scones were waiting to go in next and Sam found herself busy for twenty minutes before it finally occurred to her to wonder—how had Bobul known her name?

But when she turned to ask him, she saw that he was standing over the stove, tending a glass bowl over a pan of hot water from which the most incredible chocolate aroma emanated. Her voice didn't seem to work. She gave a quick shake of her head and turned back to her own work, trying to remember what she'd been doing three seconds earlier.

Catching sight of her desk reminded her that she'd never gotten around to placing her supply order the previous evening. She wiped her hands on a damp towel and headed for the computer at her desk.

"Will require these items." Bobul stood beside her left

shoulder, balancing the bowl of chocolate against his bulky belly with one hand and holding out a slip of paper with the other.

Sam reached for the list, ready to comment, but a glance told her that they were simple items she would be ordering anyway—sugar, butter, chocolate—although the latter was among the most expensive brands her supplier carried. When she looked up again, the chocolatier was at the work table stirring the contents of his bowl, intent upon the way the molten chocolate drizzled from his wooden spoon. She shrugged and went back to her order, finalizing it with a couple of clicks and printing out the wholesaler's confirmation page.

Trays of cookies came out of the oven and the next time Sam glanced toward Bobul, he was working a pool of melted chocolate back and forth with a spatula. As it thickened slightly he sprinkled it with something from one of his mysterious little packets, stirred again, then scooped the chocolate into a pastry bag and began dispensing it into the plastic molds. How much stuff had he brought with him anyway?

"Sam?" Jennifer peered in from the doorway. "We have a customer here for her wedding cake consultation and I've got four others waiting at the counter."

Sam handed the baked cookies off to Jen. "It's after ten. Have we heard from Becky?"

"Uh, yeah. She called awhile ago and said that the school has cancelled for the day. Something about the heat going out."

So, somebody light the pilot like I did, Sam thought as the sounds of voices came from the sales room. But there was nothing to be done about it. Busy days just happened, and usually when you were short of help. She supposed she could call Kelly in if necessary. But that would involve driving home to get her. And by the time Kelly's car was drivable again, the crush at the bakery would surely slow down. She sighed and put a smile on her face before picking up her order book and stepping out front to meet the bride.

The twenty-something girl sat at one of the bistro tables, looking like a timid rabbit next to an indomitable woman with iron gray hair and a hard stare. They introduced themselves as Miramar Southwell ("just call me Mira") and her mother, Sylvia. Sam greeted them as warmly as she could, considering the unfriendly vibes from momzilla.

"I've heard that your cakes are ridiculously expensive," the older woman began.

Then shop elsewhere. What she said was, "It all depends on what you order, Mrs. Southwell. As you can see from the selection in the display cases, some of our standard designs are very reasonable."

A whimper from the young bride let Sam know that she was certainly hoping for more.

"Did you bring pictures of what you have in mind?" Sam suggested. At Mira's blank look, Sam took another tactic. "Well, let's look through the ideas in our portfolio." She went to the counter behind the display cases, getting a sympathetic look from Jen as she passed, and retrieved the oversized folder of photos of some of her previous cakes.

After nearly an hour of hair-pulling agony, the Southwells were in agreement on nothing. Mira held out for spectacular while her mother demanded cheap. Sam wanted to make suggestions but the pair couldn't even seem to agree on how many guests they needed to feed. And the wedding was less than two weeks away. Twice, Sam left the table hoping to give them some space—or to drop the hint that she had other work to do.

A peek into the kitchen revealed Bobul at the work table, with a good-sized pile of molded chocolates in front of him. He was in the process of dusting each one with a gossamer whiff of translucent white powder, something that looked as light as a single snowflake. On doily-covered servers, he'd accumulated a collection of truffles and hand-dipped little mounds that looked mighty enticing to Sam. A growl from her stomach reminded her that she'd had about a quarter of a muffin for breakfast and that it was well past lunch time now.

The chocolatier glanced up at Sam. "Must sample," he said, noticing the way she was eyeing the tiny blocks of extra-dark.

"Thanks." She reached to take one but Bobul eased the serving plate beyond her grasp.

"This," he said, holding out one of the freshly dusted ones. "We offer this as Christmas specialty."

She thought of reminding him that there was no 'we' at this point. She'd not even verbally hired him yet. But the glisten of the rich chocolate caught her attention. The piece was molded in the shape of a pinecone, perfect down to the sharp tips at the end of each precisely fluted bract. The cup-like inner depths were reddish, tinted somehow to give even more dimension to the piece. And at the outer tips, a faint hint of gold. Each was truly a miniature work of art.

"Taste," he said, folding his arms and watching her.

She took a tentative nibble. The dark chocolate broke with the *snap* that perfectly tempered pieces should have.

The blend of flavors that hit her palate was indescribable—the bite of dark chocolate, a hint of raspberry, a breath of pure sweet—but there was something else that she couldn't quite name. The small bit dissolved on her tongue and she stared at the remainder of it in her fingers before popping it into her mouth. A moan of pure pleasure escaped.

"Is acceptable," Bobul pronounced.

Sam was pretty sure her eyes rolled back in their sockets. When she focused again, she saw that Bobul was headed for the sales room with a server balanced on each hand. She trailed along, half wanting to stop him, with the wild idea that she could keep all the exquisite chocolates for herself.

By the time she reached the outer room, he was standing at the bistro table where Sam had left mousy Mira and the overwhelming Sylvia in intense conversation. Each of them held a piece of Bobul's chocolate and Sam found herself holding her breath as they opened their mouths. Mira took a small nibble and Sam smiled as the girl's reaction mirrored her own. Sylvia popped the miniature pinecone into her mouth whole, mulled it around a little and then swallowed. Her shoulders relaxed, her head lolled to one side, and she raised it with a smile.

Sam hustled over to them as Bobul circled the room and offered samples to each of the other customers. Within moments, the room filled with exclamations and delighted whispers. Bobul deposited the serving plates on top of the nearest display case and walked back to the kitchen without another word.

Jen gave Sam a frantic signal.

"How much are we selling them for?" she whispered. "People are already wanting to buy."

"A dollar each for the large truffles? Fifty cents for the pinecones?"

Jen leaned closer to Sam's ear. "Better triple that. Believe me, no one will complain."

Sam gave a quick shrug and turned back to her bride and mom, hoping desperately to get some decisions made so she could get back to her other duties. And she *really* needed to talk to Mr. Bobul.

The pair of Southwells had their heads together and when they noticed Sam they both smiled widely.

"I love the truffles," Mira said. "I want them made up as favors for the guests. Mother and I have decided that we—"

"We're inviting the entire list. There's no point in cutting back, darling. It's your big day, after all."

Sam stared back and forth between them. Where was momzilla? Who'd replaced the tense pair she'd been working with for the past hour?

"So, Ms. Sweet," Sylvia continued. "Three hundred guest favors—I'm thinking four truffles to a box. Tied with a burgundy bow."

"And we'll repeat that same color on the cake. Burgundy and gold. Very holiday, very rich." Mira spoke with such authority that Sam had to take a look back at the mother, just to be sure there weren't about to be fireworks.

Within ten minutes Sam had the order written up for the four-tier cake and had sketched out the design as she imagined it, fondant draped, richly quilted, with gold beads and burgundy trim. And she'd collected the deposit check.

"It's going to be so beautiful, isn't it, Mom?" Mira was positively glowing as the pair walked out of the shop.

Sam watched them get into their Mercedes SUV.

Okay, what just happened here? She marched into the kitchen, determined to find out what kind of nonsense this Bobul guy was up to.

Chapter 5

The chocolatier stood at the worktable, his small fingers working a sugary purple substance into the shape of petals, forming the most delicate violets Sam had ever seen. She stared for a few seconds before she remembered why she'd come back here.

"Mr. Bobul—"

He grunted but didn't take his eyes off the tiny flower in his hand.

"Is there something . . . I mean . . . I'm trying to figure out what happened out there with Mrs. Southwell and her daughter. Those two were nearly at each others' throats until they tasted your chocolates."

He glanced at her, his eyebrows dipping together in front. "The chocolate. It having many special—how do you call it—properties."

His attention went right back to his creations and Sam saw that he was not to be diverted. She turned back to the fruitcake recipe she'd decided to try, hoping to achieve something people wouldn't consider using as a doorstop.

She'd no sooner located the card where she'd written it than Jen caught her attention with a *psst*—standing in the doorway to the sales area and signaling Sam to come speak to her.

"All the chocolates are gone, Sam. And now people are asking if we'll have gift boxes for Christmas. And gift baskets. What shall I tell them?"

Sam debated for a fraction of a minute. "Tell them yes to the boxed chocolates. And take orders for baskets. Somehow, we'll do this."

She turned back to Bobul and noticed that he'd completed a tray of elegant white chocolate truffles, each decorated with a pair of the tiny violets he'd created a few minutes ago. Displayed on a silver plate with delicately fluted edges, they took her breath away.

"Wow." She couldn't seem to come up with anything else to say.

"Is nice choice for winter or for spring," he answered, handing her the plate.

"May I?" She reached for one, practically drooling for a taste.

He held up the baking sheet on which he'd been working. "For tasting," he said. "Those for customers."

Good idea. Sam bit into the side of the white truffle, to discover that the center was a rich dark chocolate blend that literally melted the instant it touched her tongue.

"Oh my," she mumbled. She nibbled one of the sugared violets from the top, then the other. Did she merely imagine that they actually tasted like flowers? Umm . . .

It wasn't her imagination that her knees went a little weak.

Out in the sales area she heard the distinctive voice of Ivan Petrenko, the bookshop owner from next door. Uh-oh. This afternoon was his book group called Chocoholics Unanimous and Sam hadn't even begun making the peppermint brownies she'd planned for them. She glanced at the tray of truffles.

"Stay right here," she said to Gustav Bobul. "We need to talk."

She slid through the opening in the curtained doorway and waltzed up to Ivan with the beautiful silver plate.

He stared at the truffles and his breath drew in with a gasp. "Samantha!"

"Dark chocolate truffle that, I can attest, is to die for. White chocolate, hand dipped. The violets aren't technically made of choc—"

"No matter. I can promise you . . . book group will be loving them."

Two other customers looked longingly at the plate as Sam carried it to the back counter and gave it a quick cellophane wrap and signature purple bow along with a "Magical Delights" sticker. Ivan carried the prize out, as if they were the crown jewels of Russia. As he headed back to his bookshop, she murmured to the other customers, "Don't worry, there are more."

She quickly retrieved the remaining truffles from the tray in the kitchen and before she'd turned her back, Jen had sold half of them.

Back in the kitchen, Bobul was contemplating a pile

of cocoa beans that he'd evidently roasted at home and brought with him.

"Only the nibs," he said, noticing Sam's puzzled expression. "I have already to taking off the chaff. Will now grind."

Uh huh, whatever it takes.

"Look, Bobul . . . I'd like to make your employment situation permanent." It didn't take an Einstein to see that the man was good for business.

He shrugged, as if that weren't important to him. But Sam really didn't want to let this one get away. She named a figure that momentarily startled both of them.

"I'll just need to get a little information for our records, and then you'll be on the payroll."

He shifted from one foot to the other.

"You know, full name, address, social security number?"

His glance slid to the left.

"Oh. Right. Well then, green card?"

He looked puzzled.

Oh boy. "No green card?"

He shrugged his huge shoulders.

Sam's mind raced. There was no way she could duplicate the confections he'd produced. The customers were already completely hooked, Jen was out there taking orders for gift baskets and Sam couldn't let them down.

"Cash," she said. "And you can't tell anyone." Her stomach took a lurch. She could *so* be shut down for this. Dating the sheriff and hiring an illegal weren't the safest combination.

But the chocolatier had visibly relaxed.

She forced all the negatives to the back of her mind as she outlined for him the hours she wanted him to work and explained the requirement to keep quiet about their arrangement. She took a deep breath as he went back to work with a mortar and pestle, grinding the cacao beans into powder.

The sound of a truck outside in the alley caught her attention. She couldn't believe that it was already after two o'clock. She met the driver at the door and directed him where to put the new supplies while she reviewed the packing list and signed for the delivery.

A glimpse of the brilliant, clear sky reminded her about winterizing the house in Talpa which was now under her care. She really couldn't afford to be away from the bakery at this moment but there was no choice. The power was to be cut off today and by tonight the temperatures would surely drop even lower.

She checked the sales room and found that the earlier crowd had cleared. Jen had enough cookies, cheesecake and scones in the displays to tide her over through the mid-afternoon coffee break rush. Bobul seemed content at the stove, adding cream and sugar to something in a double boiler.

She would have to be careful around Beau. He was pretty smitten with her, but he was also a man of principle and she couldn't see him simply looking the other way if he figured out what was going on. And keeping secrets from him . . . it wouldn't be easy.

She put those thoughts out of her mind while she went into the hardware store to purchase a new lockset for the Talpa house. How did it all get so complicated?

* * *

Away from the center of town Sam kept the truck in four wheel drive and took the turns cautiously. Out in Talpa, it appeared that lots of folks had opted to stay in for the day. One yard was filled with kids romping in the snow and trying to make snowballs from the scant piles of slush that remained in the shaded areas. Otherwise, the neighborhood was pretty quiet. She parked once more in front of the large gate, gathered her tools and the new lockset, and walked through the smaller gate.

Her tracks from the previous night had melted away and the red tag was gone from the front door, replaced by a notice of some kind. She ripped it down and glanced at it—an emergency phone number the owner could call in order to bring the account up to date and get electricity restored. Low income customers could make arrangements for a payment plan or apply for assistance. A glance around the sizeable house and costly landscaping told Sam lack of money was probably not the issue here.

She stared again at the expensive lock on the front door. Shame to ruin it with the drill. She trudged over the brown lawn toward the back of the house. Two sets of doors faced a wide flagstone terrace. A quick perusal revealed that one of those led to a bedroom, where an unmade bed dribbled blankets and sheets off the edge and onto the tile floor, as if the owner had just risen for his or her morning coffee and hadn't yet returned to tidy the room. Thick Persian rugs gave the place a rich appearance.

Peering through the panes of the other doors she saw a

great-room, obviously made for entertaining. Large leather couches faced an oversized kiva fireplace and two other groupings of chairs made up conversation areas. Paintings hung on the wide, expansive walls. A long dining table was surrounded by high-backed carved chairs, so many of them that they disappeared into the dark distance of the room. A granite bar marked the dividing point to a kitchen that Sam could barely see.

It was this door Sam decided to drill. The process took about ten minutes, including replacing the old lock with the newly purchased one, whose keys she jammed into her coat pocket. She pushed the door open.

The whole place felt like a walk-in refrigerator. What had Delbert Crow told her about it? The mortgage was ninety days in arrears. So it may have been early September when the owners left. She walked through the rooms, finding two thermostats, both at summertime settings. She shone her flashlight into the darker corners. The house must be three thousand square feet. A library held a large ornately carved desk and a pair of leather chairs, all surrounded by floor-to-ceiling bookcases. Between the leather-bound books were bits of travel memorabilia and a few hammered silver frames with photos of smiling people in settings like ski lodges and white-sand beaches. The face that appeared in all of them was a man in his late forties with light brown hair, good looking in a breezy, almost European way. She also discovered three bedrooms—two neatly made up, formal feeling, guestrooms—the third and largest was the one she'd seen from the terrace. The one where it appeared that someone had just arisen for the day. Aside from that, nothing seemed out of place.

In the luxurious master bathroom, a man's toiletries lay

on the tile vanity top—electric razor, a comb with a couple of brown hairs stuck to it, two bottles of designer colognes. A surreptitious peek into the medicine cabinet revealed all the normal stuff, including toothbrush, deodorant and two prescription bottles. She recognized one as a blood-pressure medication. The name on both bottles was William J Montague. No sign of a female occupant.

Okay, Sam, snooping the contents of the medicine cabinet isn't part of the job of winterizing the house. She quickly closed its carved wooden door. She went back to the kitchen for a gallon of the antifreeze she'd left there and poured a bit down each of the drains in the massive bathtub, separate tiled shower, sink and toilet. She repeated the action in each of the smaller, slightly less-glamorous bathrooms.

By the time she got back to the gourmet kitchen, with its granite counters and stainless appliances, she was into her second gallon of antifreeze. As she went to pour it, she saw that the kitchen sink contained a couple of knives with food encrusted on their blades. On the breakfast bar was a bowl with a scab of dried milk and about a dozen wizened old Cheerios embedded in it. A spoon was welded to the disgusting mixture. A glass with a half-inch of suspicious orange muck at the bottom further attested to the fact that Mr. Montague had left right in the middle of his meal.

Sam checked the double-wide refrigerator, finding it full of food that was way past gone.

What on earth happened here?

Chapter 6

Sam had shoved the last of the rotten vegetables into a garbage bag when her phone rang. Fishing in her pocket for it, she saw the number of the bakery and flipped it open. She felt a guilty jolt—she hadn't meant to be gone this long.

"Sorry, Sam, I know you're busy," Jen said. "But I'm really swamped here and the new guy is no help whatsoever."

"Problems?"

"Not that so much." Jen's voice dropped to a whisper. "It's just that he keeps bringing out new stuff. All these chocolates that are just *so* beautiful. The customers are grabbing them up and I can barely keep up with that, plus the baked goods, *plus* the special orders. I hate to say it but *help!*"

"I'll get right back. I'm probably fifteen minutes away."

Jen breathed a relieved thanks and hung up. Sam called Kelly.

"Have you picked up your car yet?"

"Just now. Why? What's up?"

Sam worked as she talked, carrying the trash bag out to the front porch. "Would it be possible for you to get over to the bakery and give Jen a hand until I can get there? She's getting slammed right now." Belatedly, she thought to ask, "Have you heard anything about Iris today?"

"I haven't. I wasn't sure if I should call Beau."

"I'll call him. I can let you know. Just please head toward the bakery now."

"Yes, Mother." Kelly's jab was only half-teasing.

Sam didn't take the time to stress over her daughter. She posted the USDA notices and put one of the keys into a lockbox before dashing to her truck. She speed-dialed Beau's personal phone as she drove. His cell rang four times and went to voice mail. She left a message expressing her concern and told him to call anytime, that she'd probably be at Sweet's Sweets at least until six or so.

Kelly's red Mustang was in the alley behind the pastry shop and Sam pulled her Silverado pickup in behind it. In the kitchen, Bobul was contentedly piping some kind of red filling into molded chocolate shells.

"Hey, how's it going?" Sam asked.

He grunted some kind of positive response but didn't look up from his work. At least she had to admit that she was getting a full day's effort out of him.

"When you finish those you can go home for the day," she told him.

From the sales area came a chatter of excited voices. "Bobul?"

He looked up momentarily.

"Hey, thanks. You were absolutely right about the customers' reactions to your chocolates. I'm really glad you came along when you did."

One corner of his mouth quirked upward, the closest thing to a smile she'd seen from him yet. The little pencil mustache angled quickly upward, then back into its straight line. She thought for a minute he was going to give some kind of I-told-you-so response, but he merely picked up the molded chocolates and carried them to the refrigerator. A shriek from the front of the shop grabbed her attention.

Two women were apparently reaching for the same truffle—the last one—and Jen had attempted to step between them.

"Ladies? Is there a problem?" Sam asked.

"I saw it first," said the short Hispanic woman with a large mesh shopping bag over her arm.

"Politeness would dictate that you let me have it," responded the older woman. Kind of an age-before-beauty thing.

"We'll have more tomorrow," Sam said in the most gracious tone she could muster, considering that she'd been on her feet since five a.m.

"I want it now," demanded the older lady. "I was going to eat it on the way home."

The other woman glared at Sam. There would probably no winning this battle, but in a moment of Solomon-esque inspiration she plucked the truffle from its display plate and cut it in half. Handing each of them a piece, she said, "There. On the house this time."

They popped the treats into their mouths before Sam could change her mind, and then both of them performed the same eye-rolling moan that Sam had caught herself doing earlier in the day. They walked out of the shop like the best of friends.

"Good job, Mom," Kelly said under her breath, as she picked out two scones for another customer.

"It's been like that all day," Jen said.

"Becky should be back tomorrow," Sam said. "One of us can bake and the other will be out front with you. And I might have to think about taking on some additional help through the holidays."

"I know someone who needs a job for a short time," Kelly said, as Sam stepped from behind the counter, heading toward the bistro tables which were in need of a wipedown.

"Seriously?" Working for mom was usually pretty low on most younger people's list of ambitions.

"Well, depending on how Iris is doing by now. Beau said there would be time in the hospital and then a rehab place for her. I just got the feeling . . ."

Neither of them wanted to finish the thought that his mother's medical care could go long-term.

Sam gathered used cups and carried them to the sink in the kitchen. No sign of Bobul. It was a little weird how he showed up and vanished without a sound. But she had a lot more on her mind at the moment.

Kelly finished cleaning the tables and Jen rearranged the display cases. For the first time all day, the shop was empty and relatively quiet. Until Sam's phone rang.

She reached into her pocket and pulled it out. Beau.

"Hey, how are things going today?" she asked, walking out to the privacy of the sunny front sidewalk.

"Well, I'm as whupped as an old dog, but Mama's doing

a little better."

"I'm glad. Kelly will be relieved to hear it."

"It's gonna be awhile, Sam. I don't know what to tell Kelly about the job. Tending my animals is hardly worth the drive for her. I wish I could afford to pay her full time while Mama's doing all the rehab and stuff, but our insurance isn't going to cover a lot of this stuff."

"Beau, don't worry." She explained about the need for holiday help at the bakery. "If you need her back before Christmas, I'm sure we can manage. If not, well, I can keep her busy so she won't go out and find another job."

He chuckled. "That almost sounds like a little conspiracy."

She pictured his ocean blue eyes and the way his face crinkled when he smiled. Her stomach got that fluttery feeling, and it wasn't because she hadn't eaten any lunch.

"I can explain it to her. Hey, would you like to come over for dinner tonight? It's going to be something really simple—probably spaghetti with sauce from a jar. I don't have the energy for much else."

"*Nothing* else?" he teased.

She got a flash of him naked and felt a tiny surge. But it quickly faded.

"Well, I'm assuming you'll need to get right back to the hospital. But even if you didn't, I don't know how long I'm good for this world once I sit down tonight."

"Sounds like you've got a lot on your mind."

"That's putting it mildly. There's a new, uh, product we've just introduced." She caught herself, just short of mentioning Bobul.

He didn't seem to notice. "Dinner, even bottled spaghetti sauce, sounds great. What time?"

"Seven?"

She walked back into the sales area to find a trio of young girls ogling the chocolate chip cookies and a woman with a toddler who was explaining to Jen that she needed a quick dessert because her mother-in-law had just informed her that she'd be coming for dinner. Kelly took care of the girls, and Jen was making a strong case for the final Yule log cake that remained in the display.

With things under control here, Sam went back to the kitchen to wash up the utensils, half expecting that Bobul might have left her with a sinkful of chocolate coated pots and pans. She was pleasantly surprised to see that he'd washed and stacked all the bowls and implements he'd used. The packets of seasonings and his bag of roasted cacao beans were out of sight. The kitchen itself showed no trace that he'd worked there all day.

She gave a little head-shake.

Half questioning her sanity, Sam went to the large walk-in refrigerator and yanked the door open. The chocolate molds he'd been working on twenty minutes ago were not there.

Chapter 7

She'd specifically watched Bobul place those molds in the fridge. What the heck was going on here? The odd feeling that maybe she'd dreamed the entire day and had just awakened to a different reality flicked through her mind.

Then she spotted the molds on one of the utility shelves, safe inside a clear plastic storage bin. Of course he wouldn't leave them in the fridge overnight. The chocolate would get too cold and be ruined. He'd probably placed them in there to harden while he washed the dishes, then he'd put them for safe keeping overnight where she'd just found them.

You're getting too tired, Sam. The late, practically sleepless night, the early morning, trying to keep track of the shop and her caretaking job and now Beau's mother and the weather. *Tonight,* she promised herself, *will be an early bedtime.*

"Mom?" Kelly sounded faintly impatient. "Where were you just now? Some other planet?"

"I guess." Sam sighed and straightened a couple of items on the shelves.

"I called out three times before you heard me. You're pooped. Why don't you go on home, leave Jen and me to close up the shop?"

Sam glanced at the clock above the sink. It was after five. "You're right. I am and I will."

"Want me to bring something for dinner?"

"No, that's okay. I thought just spaghetti and a simple salad—we have everything at home. Beau's coming over."

"Did he say anything about how Iris is doing?"

"She's a little better today. I guess he can fill us in later." Sam left her baker's jacket on a hook and pulled on her winter coat. "See you at home soon."

It wasn't until she approached her truck that she remembered she'd tossed two bags of rotten food from the Talpa house into the back and in her rush to get back to the bakery had forgotten all about them. She quickly deposited them in the alley dumpster and pulled out onto the street.

Zoë. Sam had completely forgotten that she'd planned to meet with her friend this afternoon and get the recipes for some Jewish holiday treats. Pausing a little too long at a stop sign she got honked at.

"Okay, okay," she muttered, pulling through the intersection and edging to the side so the impatient man could go around.

Tired as she felt at this moment, she didn't know that there would be any better time. Besides, Zoë had probably gone to some effort for this. Zoë and her husband Darryl lived at their bed-and-breakfast, in a big territorial style house, only a few blocks from Sam's place so she simply turned left off Kit Carson Road.

"Hey you," Zoë greeted at the kitchen door. "Come on in."

Sam wiped her feet on the mat, glancing around in the deepening dusk. An avid gardener, Zoë had carefully bedded down her plants for the winter and her back deck looked neat and organized.

"It's really getting cold out," Zoë said. "How about a cup of chai?"

Sam wanted to plead a zillion projects and just get home but she saw the look on Zoë's face. She and her best friend hadn't spent much quality time in recent weeks.

"Sure. Chai sounds wonderful." She slipped out of her jacket while Zoë checked the kettle that stayed warm over a low burner all day. While her friend turned up the flame and the water began to make bubbling sounds, Sam noticed a folder on the tiled breakfast bar. She touched the old-fashioned flowered design on the front of it.

"That was my grandmother's recipe file," Zoë said, spooning chai mix into two mugs. "Funny, the things we remember from childhood. My mother and dad moved to the commune before I was born. I don't recall that we observed any religious holidays at all. Darryl and I . . . well, we're just these earth-child types who go along with whatever our friends are doing."

She carried two steaming mugs to the counter and hitched herself up onto one of the bar stools. "But this little recipe folder . . . I remember Grandma Steiger would pull out this thing and page through it when I would visit her in the summers. She'd find traditional Jewish things to make. Said I shouldn't lose the old ways."

Her gaze grew distant.

"That's nice," Sam said. "Of course I grew up with Texas home-cooking, and I'll never think of any holiday as complete without pecan pie."

"I'm afraid I really have drifted away from those old ways. I don't know that I've ever baked any of these recipes. But you are certainly welcome to try them." She shoved the folder toward Sam.

"I'll make copies and get these back to you. Even if you never make the recipes, the memories are important to you."

Zoë nodded absently, sipping her chai. Silence filled a few more moments.

"So, how are things with the handsome sheriff?" Zoë finally asked, with a little smile. She'd been one of Sam's strong supporters when the new romance started up.

"Oh, gosh, I completely forgot to tell you." Sam quickly filled her friend on the developments with Iris over the past twenty-four hours. "As a result, Beau has been at the hospital nearly the whole time. He's coming over for a quick dinner tonight, but I'm sure he'll have to get right back. In fact . . ." She glanced at the digital clock on Zoë's stove. "He'll be there and Kelly will be home from the store in about a half hour. I better get going."

As it turned out, Kelly was already home and pacing the kitchen floor when Sam walked in.

"I thought you were coming straight from the bakery. I was getting worried."

Sam marveled at what a little mom Kelly could be— shades of herself years ago when Kelly was the kid, getting home late from some after-school activity.

"Sorry. I forgot to tell you that I needed to stop at

Zoë's." She held up the recipe folder. "More homework for me."

Kelly gave her mother an indulgent smile. "Always learning something new, aren't you?"

"Hey, it's healthy for me. Can't just settle back and let all these gray hairs take over my life."

"You'll never do that, Mom." She reached into the fridge for salad ingredients. "So, what's the story with the new guy at the shop and all the candy? Jen said it was a madhouse there all day."

Sam pulled out her large pasta pot and ran water into it at the sink. As they worked, she filled Kelly in on the strange appearance of Bobul and his amazing talent with chocolate—everything except for the fact that she'd worked out the little cash-under-the-table deal. Kelly couldn't always keep a secret, and she did work for Beau. At some point, though, Sam was going to have to figure out a solution. She didn't want to lose her chocolatier, but she knew she couldn't have a romantic relationship with secrets.

Beau's headlights beamed through the kitchen window as his Explorer swung down the long driveway and into a parking spot next to Sam's truck.

"Whoa—getting cold out there!" he said as he stepped into the service porch. "Forecast is for single-digits."

Kelly was stirring the sauce on the stove and Sam took the moment to slip her arms inside Beau's sheepskin jacket. He indulged her with a long kiss.

"Um, better."

"All right, you two. Dinner's almost ready." Kelly carried the large salad bowl to the table, where she'd already set three places.

Sam drained the pasta and poured wine while the others

began to fill their plates. The room grew quiet for a few minutes as they started eating. Sam was just taking her first sip of wine when her phone rang. She glanced at the readout and saw that it was Delbert Crow.

"I'll call him back later," she said.

"New caretaking job?" Beau asked.

"Yeah, a strange one. In fact," she said, picking up a square of garlic bread, "I meant to ask you if you know anything about this place." She described the property in Talpa. "The occupant's name is William Montague. Well, at least that's the name on some prescription bottles I found there."

"He abandoned his house but left his meds behind?"

"And more. It doesn't look like he's moved out. The place is fully furnished, and with good pieces. Most of the house was as neat as if the housekeeper had just left, but there were so many inconsistencies."

She passed the salad bowl to Beau for seconds. "I mean, if this guy took an extended trip, why were his personal things lying out on the bathroom vanity? Why would he leave so much food in the fridge? Why wouldn't the bed be made up? Even if he had a travel bag with duplicates of the toiletries, he surely had to take his blood pressure medication with him."

"Maybe he had duplicate bottles of that too?" Kelly suggested.

Sam looked toward Beau, eyebrows raised. He merely shrugged.

"I just don't think it looks right. I've been doing this for a few years, and yes sometimes I walk into places that are fully furnished. But it's usually because someone died and there were no relatives to come clean out their possessions.

Or because somebody is a jump ahead of the law and they skipped out fast."

"And there was that hoarder's place awhile back," Beau reminded her.

"Well, yeah. That lady couldn't have gotten her furniture out through the clutter if she'd tried." She paused for another sip of her wine. "But this place just doesn't feel like that. The guy obviously has money. You'd agree if you saw the quality of the things in that house. Why wouldn't he just keep his mortgage up, pay in advance or something if he planned to be away?"

Beau set his fork down. "Well, darlin', if I may offer a little lesson in real life . . . and please don't take this the wrong way . . . but there are people who live the rich life who have not an extra penny to their names. Do you know how many people are in hock up to their eyeballs? Absolutely everything they have is bought on credit? Cards maxed out, second and third mortgages?"

Sam met his gaze. He truly wasn't being preachy. "I know. And you're right." She tapped her foot against the leg of her chair. "I just . . . I don't know how to explain it."

"Well, to answer your first question, I haven't heard anything about this Montague guy, but I'll keep my ears open." He wiped his mouth on a napkin and pushed his chair back. "Hate to eat and run, but I better call this an early night."

Kelly inquired about Iris as Beau carried dishes to the sink.

"A little better today, hon. We still don't know how long a recovery we're in for, I'm afraid." He pulled his sheepskin jacket from the hook where he left it. "I'll let you know if we hear anything new."

Sam reached for a small bin on the counter where she stashed spare things from the bakery. "If you don't mind having day-old, I can send some cupcakes with you."

"Just one," he said with a smile. "Gotta watch my waistline and having a girlfriend with a bakery isn't helping."

"Take them to the office then," she said. "I know some of those guys aren't watching their figures."

He laughed out loud. "You got that right."

She folded one of her bakery boxes and carefully placed a dozen chocolate cupcakes with buttercream frosting and peppermint flakes on them. "A little holiday spirit for the guys."

His vehicle wound its way out of her driveway and down the lane and Sam watched it disappear into the frosty night. Kelly had the dishwasher loaded by the time Sam stepped back inside from the service porch, and she reminded Sam of the call she'd missed during dinner.

"Right. I better call him back before it gets any later." She dialed the number from memory and sat down at her desk, leaning back in her chair and closing her eyes while the phone rang.

"Just checking to see if you got that new property winterized," Crow said after she greeted him.

She assured him that she'd done her duties and described the mysterious things she'd noticed—the crusty dishes, the unmade bed and other signs of a hasty exit.

"I don't know, Sam. I'm only going by my paperwork, and it only tells me that the mortgage wasn't paid." Mr. Friendly, as usual.

Sam went to bed that night with a hundred questions plaguing her.

Chapter 8

Despite the rocky start to her night's rest, Sam must have fallen into a deep sleep because she woke to the beeping of her alarm, feeling as if she'd only put her head on the pillow minutes earlier. She stretched luxuriously and sat up. For a moment she felt completely at ease, but then she remembered it all—the new chocolatier, the stack of holiday orders, the fact that Kelly would now be working for her, and the nagging questions about that large, luxurious adobe house, abandoned.

She gave one more indulgent stretch, rolled her shoulders and headed for the bathroom. A steaming shower and a few extra minutes to massage conditioner into her hair made her wish she had the luxury of bundling into a robe and spending the morning with a good book. She couldn't remember the last time she'd indulged in that particular favorite pastime. The pastry shop was closed on Sundays, and she promised herself she would truly take the time off this weekend—away from all other concerns.

She dressed by the soft lamplight in her bedroom, taking a few extra minutes with the blow dryer so her hair wouldn't be damp when she went out into the frigid outdoors. Her mother's words always came back, the oft-repeated caution about catching your death of cold if you went out with wet hair. Silly, she thought, flipping the soft layers with her brush. Any scientist or doctor would tell you that colds were caused by viruses, not the weather. But she dried it anyway—old habit.

Her wooden jewelry box sat on the dresser, dark and cold now. Sam almost felt guilty, as if she'd not paid enough attention to it recently, as if the strange carved box had a personality. She lifted the lid and took out her favorite earrings. The box didn't react. She picked it up, holding it at arm's length, with both hands. Heat began to seep into her hands, almost like holding them out to the fireplace to take the chill off. When she tucked it into the crook of her arm, the wood took on a golden glow and the warmth immediately suffused her entire upper body.

"Enough of that." She set the box back on the dresser, noticing that the stones of green, blue and red that were mounted in its surface were taking on a glow of their own.

She rubbed her hands against her pant legs and shook them. "You are not some kind of a pet. You are not my friend. You are not going to affect me this way."

The box's glow wavered, dimmer and brighter.

She'd experienced unimaginable things since taking possession of this object—the ability to see things other people couldn't, some kind of strange healing touch, intuitive observations of people's emotions, energy almost inhuman.

It unnerved her.

She opened a drawer in the dresser and set the box inside, closing it away from her view. Forcing her attention back to the present, Sam walked into the kitchen and started the coffee maker. Although she normally grabbed her first cup at the bake shop, her daughter would probably want a caffeine jolt the minute she woke up. They'd agreed that Kelly would come in for work when Sweet's Sweets opened at seven. Meanwhile, Sam knew that the shop couldn't open until she provided something for the customers to buy.

The frozen ground crunched under her feet as she walked out to her truck. The big Silverado cranked to life immediately. Sam had come close to selling it last summer; now she was glad she hadn't.

The alley behind Sweet's Sweets sat in darkness, dimly illuminated by the glow of the one streetlamp at the end of the block. Sam fumbled her key into the ice-cold lock and didn't see Gustav Bobul until he spoke.

"Good morning, Miss Sam."

"Bobul! You startled me!" She patted at her thumping heart.

He didn't respond, merely waited patiently with that bulging canvas bag across his chest until she got the door open and the lights switched on. She covered her irritation at his silent appearance by bustling through her startup routine—turning on the bake oven, pulling butter from the refrigerator to soften, putting on her baker's jacket. When she turned back toward him, she noticed a faint smile on his face.

"Is gift for you, Miss Sam," he said. He pointed with one of his delicate hands at an object he'd set on the work table.

Crafted in chocolate, it was a rectangular box about three inches on the longest side. The surface was covered with criss-crossed diagonal lines, giving it a quilted appearance. Uncannily like her wooden box at home.

"What's this, Bobul?"

"Is gift. See? Lid come off." He reached out and opened the little box. Inside were some tiny objects.

"No, I mean what *is* this? This shape, the pattern on it, the lid. What did you base it on?"

He shrugged, clearly not understanding the question.

Oh, never mind. He watched expectantly. "It's lovely, Bobul. A very pretty chocolate creation."

"Bobul can make these for shop. Customers will like. Can put things in."

Sam peered into the hollow interior of the chocolate box. The items he'd placed inside were fashioned of chocolate. Painted with edible gold dust, they resembled jewelry.

She stared at him but he only seemed eager that she appreciate the gift.

"It's nice, Bobul, and I'll think about adding them to the shop. But for now, we need more of the types of chocolates you made yesterday. I'm going to order gift boxes so we can sell assortments of your pieces."

He gave a quick nod and placed his bag beside the table then hurried to retrieve the molded chocolates he'd made the previous afternoon. By the time Sam got her first batches of muffins and scones into the oven, he'd covered the table top with bowls and paraphernalia and was happily melting a new pot of chocolate at the stove.

The tiny chocolate box sat out of harm's way on her desk. She sat down to order the gift boxes they would need for the new chocolate assortments but her eyes kept drifting from her computer screen to the little box. Could it be pure coincidence that it looked so much like the wooden box with the strange powers? The box given to her by a supposed witch?

Sam discreetly laid a sheet of paper over the distracting object and got back to her order. With a couple of online searches beyond her normal packaging suppliers she came up with two sizes of containers, estimating that one would accommodate a half-pound of assorted chocolates and the other would work for a one-pound selection. The boxes were covered in an icy pink iridescent paper that would coordinate beautifully with her signature purple embossed labels. Or, a red holiday bow would really set off the special look. She spotted deeper boxes with unique fold-down tops, which would be perfect for the sets of four truffles for Mira Southwell's wedding, Sam double checked her shopping cart and placed the order.

At some point while she'd been engrossed with the computer order, the muffins had come out of the oven. Bobul must have removed them and set the pans into the cooling racks. Sam brought them out and drizzled vanilla glaze over the tops of cranberry-orange muffins, then gave a shake of snowy powdered sugar to the apple-cinnamon ones and carried them out to the display cases in the sales room. A tap on the front window caught her attention.

"Riki, hi!" she said, letting the owner of the neighboring business inside. The curly-haired British woman who hardly outweighed some of the dogs she groomed, scooted in and gave Sam a hug.

"I'm so glad I spotted you," she said. "I've been dying for a scone to go with my breakfast tea. Are there any?"

"One minute. I just finished blueberry and some cherry-amaretto. Of course you can also just get a plain one."

"Ooh, the cherry-amaretto would be brilliant!"

"Sorry the coffee isn't on yet. Kelly and Jen should be here any time, to really get everything set up."

"No problem. My pot of tea is ready. I've got twenty minutes before my first poodle comes in this morning. Wait, you said Kelly is working here now?"

That led to the whole explanation about Beau and his mother's situation as Sam carried a tray of scones to the front. Upon seeing them Riki couldn't narrow down her choice and ended up taking one of each flavor. Sam had just closed the door behind her when she heard voices from the back. Evidently the whole staff was here.

Jen and Kelly chattered away as they put on their shop aprons and bustled to the front, setting up the coffee service, turning on lights, making sure they were ready for customers. Bobul already had a good-sized plate of finished truffles—these dipped in dark chocolate and decorated with tiny winter designs—detailed crystalline snowflakes, striped candy canes and Christmas trees fashioned of chocolate. How did the large man create such captivating miniatures?

"These are amazing, Bobul. Are they ready for the customers?"

"*Da,* Miss Sam. And here are some more." He held out the molded chocolates he'd begun the night before. A marbled red vein swirled across the top of each piece, making the firm squares look as if they'd been chiseled from a block of dark stone.

Sam hustled the delicacies out to the sales area. "Cut a couple of these truffles into small pieces for samples."

She caught Kelly eyeing the candy with a greedy eye. "Samples for the customers," she reminded firmly. "Jen, you keep an eye on her."

Back in the kitchen, Sam checked her stack of custom orders for the day. As soon as Becky came in, she could start baking cake layers and creating some of the simpler frosting decorations like roses. Meanwhile, Sam stirred up two of their more popular coffee cake recipes and got them into the oven for the morning crowd. As they baked, she consulted the folder Zoë had given her and performed calculations to triple some of the Jewish cookie recipes.

"Is a good kitchen you have here," Bobul said, watching as Sam took the spice-filled coffee cakes from the oven.

"It's nice working with good equipment, that's for sure," she answered.

"No . . . not what I mean. Is good how fast Miss Sam work. Turn out the best . . . what is word? . . . quality. Top quality in fast time. Almost like magic."

She looked up, searching for a hint of knowledge in his face. But he had turned away, his back to her as he stirred a pan of chocolate on the stove. What was it about this guy? Could it be purely coincidental that he'd made a chocolate box that was nearly an exact miniature of her own, and then the little hints . . .? No, she had to chalk it up to being overly sensitive about his presence.

The back door opened before she had a chance to say anything more. Her baking assistant, Becky came in on a gust of chill air.

"Good morning. Sam. Sorry that I couldn't come in yesterday. I'll get right to—" Her voice broke off when she noticed Bobul at the stove and she turned to Sam with an expression full of questions.

"Becky, meet Gustav Bobul, our new chocolatier."

He gave her a quick nod and turned back to his work.

"I . . . uh . . . Nice to meet you."

"Jen convinced me that our customers were interested in chocolates and if yesterday's sales were any indication . . . well, I'd say she was right." Sam ushered Becky through the connecting curtain.

A quick look at the new offerings and Sam brought Becky's attention back to the cake and pastry orders for the day. Two children's birthday cakes needed to be finished before noon, then she wanted to experiment with the new Hanukkah recipes in addition to filling the displays with a solid assortment of Santas, wreaths and trees. The best thing, Sam had discovered, about hiring Becky was that she worked efficiently, with a minimum of direction. Soon, the scent of cake layers filled the kitchen.

Sam was in the midst of cutting poinsettia leaves from red-tinted chocolate when Jen's voice came over the intercom.

"Sheriff Cardwell is here, Sam. Would you like to come out, or should I send him back?"

She glanced at Bobul. "I'll be right there."

Beau in uniform always took her breath away. She still had a hard time getting over the fact that this man who could easily be posing for sexy cologne ads would be interested in her, the chubby baker with no makeup, whose hair always seemed to be in need of a trim. It was probably the most endearing thing about him, the fact that he saw through most people's superficiality and was more interested in a genuine relationship. His smile lit up when he spotted her and she resisted the urge to check her clothing for flour smudges and dabs of frosting.

"How is Iris this morning?"

"I was just telling Kelly, she's better. There is movement now on her left side and she's starting to work at talking. The doctor is very encouraged." Beau squeezed Sam's hand. "And me, at least I'm back at work now."

"I need to go by and see her."

"She's not real perky yet, but we'll take a day at a time. Look, I wanted to let you know that I did a little background on that Montague guy you were asking about." They walked to a quiet corner and sat at one of the tables. "There's not much. He's got no criminal record. Bought that house about fifteen years ago. As far as I could tell, he's never filed a complaint and no one has filed one against him. I'd have to go deeper to find out anything about his credit rating or any of that. And you'd need more than simple curiosity to get into those records anyway."

"Sure. I understand." Sam fiddled with a wooden stir stick. "I need to just let go of this. It's really none of my business why he left abruptly. Worrying that something might have happened to him isn't really my department, is it? I'm only supposed to take care of the house."

"That's right," he said, standing up. "Meanwhile, I need to get back to w——" He stopped in front of the display of Bobul's chocolates. "Wow, these are nice. I didn't know you made chocolates too."

Sam felt the blood rush to her face. "We're having someone else do them." That much was true.

But Beau had turned toward the door. With a quick

wave to the girls, he walked out to his cruiser.

Sam gave a sigh of relief and completely immersed herself in her work after Beau left. Cakes left for birthday parties, cookies and biscotti met up with afternoon shoppers looking for a short break in their perusal of the galleries, and two batches of cookie dough chilled in the fridge, waiting to be rolled out and cut into holiday shapes.

By the time Sam took a deep breath and looked up, it was nearing four o'clock and she could already sense the sky darkening and the night chill returning.

"I better run by that house in Talpa and be sure all the pipes held last night," she told Kelly.

"Is this for sale?" Kelly asked, holding up the little chocolate box Bobul had given Sam that morning. The chocolatier had his back turned as he worked at the sink.

Sam glanced at her daughter. "Mmm . . . sure." She slipped on her warm coat. "Can you help Jen close up, then bring the bank bag home for me?"

"It already looks like a good day," Kelly said, placing the little chocolate box into a bag. She pointed out that all the chocolates were once again gone, along with a good portion of the baked goods.

"Excellent." Sam reiterated with Bobul that the bakery would be closed on Sunday but that he should come in early Monday morning.

She drove through town with her truck window halfway down, the frigid air bracing her after the long hours near the warmth of the bake ovens. The sun had been out all day leaving only a trickle of brownish water heading toward the storm drains. At the big adobe house in Talpa, the front lawn was completely clear. Surprisingly green blades of grass poked through the brown. Another cold night and they, too, would surely retreat for the winter.

Remembering her flashlight, Sam let herself in the back door with her new key. She aimed the light at the pipes under the kitchen sink and was relieved to find no wet spots. The two guest bathrooms were similarly clear and she headed for the master bedroom and bath. Plumbing seemed intact there as well. Maybe she could just ignore the place now and let the wheels of procedure take over. There would be foreclosure papers and probably more—she wasn't exactly sure what all would happen.

The thought that no one might be in the house for months gave rise to the idea that maybe she should close all the drapes, prevent curious types from being able to see inside quite so easily. She crossed the bedroom toward the French doors. Then something crunched under her foot.

She looked down. Broken glass. Blue. She shined the flashlight at the shards. Some kind of small object—maybe a vase—must have fallen from the end table on this side of the bed and crashed to the tile floor, missing the edge of the rug at the bedside. She squatted and poked at them with her index finger. The blankets and sheets still trailed to the floor, and Sam got a weird feeling that someone had held onto them, dragging them away forcefully. Could there have been a struggle of some sort?

She closed her eyes and calmed her mind, then opened them again and tried to let images come to her. Sometimes it worked, especially after she'd handled the wooden box. But not today. She'd picked it up this morning, but that was hours ago and she got no clear impressions now.

Still, something wasn't right. Maybe if she could just

find someone related to the owner, let them know that the house was empty and that a family member should take care of it. She gave up, gathered the broken shards, and dropped them into a nearby wastebasket.

The late afternoon sun came at the house from the opposite side now, leaving the bedroom feeling shadowed and gloomy. She used her flashlight to get a quick peek into each of the nightstand drawers but didn't come across an address book or anything helpful. There'd been a study down the hall, she remembered, so she headed that direction.

The large desk stood in a bright shaft of light, the western window providing the day's final illumination. A printer sat on a small table beside it, cables dangling to the floor, no computer in sight. Had it been that way on her previous visit? Sam took a seat in the large leather-covered chair and started with the top drawer. Pens, paperclips and a host of little office junk filled that one. The second drawer contained hanging file folders but it would take awhile in the gloomy light to page through all of them. None were conveniently labeled "Names and Addresses of Family Members" so she went on.

A center drawer, the one her father always called the 'belly drawer' in his own desk, finally yielded an address book. She flipped through a few pages but found no listings on the M page where she might have found additional Montagues. With the light fading fast, she decided to take it home for further study.

Technically, she should enter the item on her sign-in sheet to notify the USDA that she'd removed property from the house, but she only intended to keep it overnight. She tucked the small book into the pocket of her coat and started to close the drawer when something else caught her eye.

Shining the flashlight into the dark rear corner of the drawer, Sam felt her breath catch. A photograph with slightly curled corners sat on top of a pair of scissors. She stared at it. The object in the picture was all too familiar to her. It was her own wooden box, the one given to her by Bertha Martinez—reputed witch.

Chapter 9

Sam's fingers trembled as she plucked the photograph from the drawer, dropping it on the desk top as if it were on fire. Her heart pounded as she stared at it.

It had to be the same box—that hand carved piece with the quilted pattern, the cabochon stones mounted at the criss-crossed lines, the ugly yellowish color of the varnish. How many of them could possibly exist?

She studied the picture until the sun abruptly dipped behind the western horizon, leaving the room in deep gloom. Suddenly the house felt too remote, too abandoned and Sam herself felt too vulnerable. She grabbed up the picture and stuck it into her pocket alongside the address book. Her legs felt a little shaky when she stood up but she pushed herself to get moving.

Abandoning the plan to circuit the place and close all the drapes, she headed through the great room and out to the back yard, took the shortest route to the road and unlocked her truck with trembling hands. Inside, she locked the doors again and told herself to get out—now. The truck roared a little too heartily when she put it in gear, but it felt good to be in motion.

Half a mile later, Sam began to feel a little foolish. After all, it was apparent that no one had been in that house for months. Why would somebody show up now, at just the moment she'd helped herself to a couple of items? And what made her so sure the photo was really of the same box that she now owned? Really, she chided herself, there could be a zillion of them—probably made in India by the hundreds.

By the time she pulled into her own driveway she'd almost convinced herself.

* * *

All evening, the address book and photograph were practically steaming their way out of her coat pocket, but she didn't trust herself to simply bring them out into the light, to share the items with Kelly. Her daughter would undoubtedly think she was crazy, and the one thing of which Sam felt certain—she wasn't crazy. At least not yet.

Finally, Kelly went to bed, commenting that she planned to sleep "forever" because it was Sunday morning. Alone at last, Sam took the book and photo from her coat and carried them to the kitchen table where she turned the overhead light to the brightest setting.

The picture was an old one. That much was evident by

the slightly fuzzy edges of the images, the lack of color brilliance that marked modern digital photography. But the box shown in the image was definitely hers—or its identical twin. It had been shot in what Sam thought of as the box's 'quiet' mode, the way it looked before she touched it, without the glow that took over the wood and the stones—the 'live' mode.

In the photo the box sat on a table. The indoor background was dark. Not black, but very muted. She turned the photo, letting the light hit it at different angles. Small figures of some kind showed up on the wall behind the object. Sam got up and rummaged in a kitchen drawer for the magnifying glass she remembered stashing there.

Under its amplification she caught her breath. The images were white figures painted on dark red walls. Walls that Sam knew.

The picture was taken in a room at the home of Bertha Martinez. When the old woman had thrust the box into Sam's hands, just before she died, her home was one of the properties temporarily under Sam's care through her USDA contract. After the dead woman's body was removed, Sam's job was to clean and empty the house so it could be sold. She vividly remembered the red room, the window covered in opaque drapes, the occult objects, the pentagram of white stones on the floor.

Sam's inquiries about Bertha Martinez revealed that the elderly woman had been considered by many to be a *bruja*, a witch of sorts. *Brujas* were reputed to be able to cast spells, and to be shape shifters. According to the legends a *bruja* would often assume the shape of an owl, taking to the air on moonlit nights, spying on mortals below. Beau had laughed it off, and Sam's natural skepticism put the whole story in the league with fairy tales, a sort of Southwestern version of something the Brothers Grimm would have thought up.

All Sam knew for certain was that from the moment she'd opened that box, while sitting right here at this kitchen table, strange things had happened to her. From the powerful, almost electrical jolt that overwhelmed her when she first touched the inner edges of the box, to the healing touch she'd inadvertently used on her best friend Zoë, to the vivid auras she'd seen surrounding people a few weeks ago after a friend died—the box contained immense power. Bertha's dying words left Sam feeling that she'd been instilled with a sacred trust to care for the box and use its power wisely.

She wished she knew something more of its history. Was it carved by an artisan here in Taos? Or had it come from some faraway place?

Now it appeared that others knew about the box. To what lengths would someone go to possess it? Far enough to kill William Montague because he had a picture of it? Could Bertha herself have been the target of some plot? Something had to account for her insistence that Sam take the box and safeguard it.

Sam dropped the photo back on the table and picked up the address book. Was Montague acquainted with Bertha Martinez? She had a feeling about the answer, but looked anyway. No listing under the letter M. Earlier, at his house, she'd glanced at that page in search of Montague relatives; Bertha's name would have sprung out at her.

Starting at the beginning of the book, which had small tabs for the letters of the alphabet and places for multiple entries on the sheets behind each tab, Sam paged through, looking for any familiar name. Montague was apparently well-connected in Taos—the book contained addresses for a former mayor and several people Sam recognized as the ubiquitous chairs of committees, charities and fundraisers. Not one of them seemed likely to be connected to an old *bruja* or a wooden box with magical powers.

The neat printing and ruled lines began to swim before her eyes and Sam realized that she'd been awake for twenty hours now and that her brain was only capable of absorbing so much. She closed the book, sticking the photograph inside the front cover, and carried it to her room.

She barely remembered brushing her teeth and falling into bed. With her puffy comforter pulled close to her chin she drifted in and out of dreams about Bertha Martinez, the occult red room, and a scene at a party in which all the important people of Taos got into an argument over the wooden box and which of them would own Sam's soul if they were to win possession of the box.

When she fought her way back to consciousness and looked at her bedside clock it was only 2:14. She worked at clearing her mind of the ridiculous dreams but her thoughts remained unsettled. The harder she concentrated, the more wakeful she became. Finally, when the numerals informed her that it was 3:29 she gave up on the pretense of sleep. She pulled on her thickest robe and fuzzy slippers and trudged toward the kitchen, switching on a living room lamp and picking up the novel she'd been wanting to read.

A cup of hot chocolate and some non-threatening literary fiction should take her mind off everything else, she decided. The kettle began to steam and the words on the first page of the book made no sense at all. She poured hot water over the powdered cocoa mix in her mug and gave it an absent stir. Back in the living room, her roiling thoughts refused to recede and she laid the book aside. With her cup of cocoa and a woolen coverlet over her legs, she nestled into the sofa's deep cushions.

She'd just begun to feel drowsy when a tap at the front window threw her heartbeat into overdrive. Every ominous portent from her earlier dreams rushed in at her. She whipped aside the coverlet and grabbed up the length of pipe that she kept near the door.

"Sam? Are you up?" The whispered voice came through the crack at the doorjamb, right where she'd pressed her ear.

She switched on the porch light and looked through the peephole. Rupert Penrick, her insomniac writer friend, stood on the porch, shivering in a flowing purple garment of some kind.

"What on earth are you doing here?" she asked as she flung the door open, realizing that was sort of an ungracious question.

"Couldn't sleep, saw your lights." He floated into the room, all two-hundred-plus pounds of him, his collar-length gray hair looking as impeccable as always. "I got to page 399 and I'm simply stumped for an ending."

"Come on in," Sam said. "I'm a little sleepless myself tonight. Hot chocolate?"

He eyed the dregs in her mug, figured out that it was the instant kind, and declined. What was she thinking?—Rupert was one of those gourmet types who made everything from scratch. Rumor was that he'd never eaten a fast-food meal.

"I have tea . . ."

"Lovely." He followed her into the kitchen and picked through her assortment of teas while she relit the flame under the kettle. "So . . . I've got my heroine up in the high turret of a castle, with one of her lovers drowning in the moat and the other locked in mortal combat with the dark knight. Can't decide which one she'll choose, and how to get rid of the other one."

Sam knew from experience that Rupert didn't truly want an answer to the question. His own preference might be to send the two lovers away together and let the poor woman in the tower fend for herself.

"And you were out walking on a sub-freezing night, looking for the solution to that?"

"Walking? Surely you jest, girl. I'd just jumped in the Land Rover to see if the all-night market had any decent Rocky Road in stock. Don't know why, but I took your street as a shortcut."

She poured water into a china teapot and searched for the silver tea strainer she'd not seen since Rupert's last visit. While he spooned a generous amount of India Passionfruit into the pot, she handed him the matching china cup and saucer and then dumped another packet of powdered cocoa mix into her mug. She located a tray, loaded it with the beverages and a plate of her own bakery cookies, and carried it to the living room.

"So, Samantha, what is it that's keeping you awake this early Sunday morning? I know for a fact that you aren't one for early rising and that this *is* your only day off from the lovely bake shop."

Sam picked up her cocoa and sank back into her corner of the sofa with a sigh, while Rupert poured his tea and doctored it with milk.

"It seems I'm smack in the middle of another mysterious . . . *thing* . . . at one of my properties."

"*Thing*. Does that mean love, murder or some other complexity of the human condition?"

"I actually don't know." She told him about the new property, embellishing a bit of detail about the gourmet kitchen, the high-end furnishings and even the expensive personal articles the owner had left behind in the bathroom—because she knew Rupert's taste for the lavish, but mainly because she knew he would question her for specifics anyway. "Aside from the broken vase in the bedroom, the refrigerator full of spoiled food, and the fact that the man has let his bills go unpaid for months . . . I don't really know that there is any mystery to it."

Rupert's mouth twisted to one side.

"Okay, there is a little more to it. In his desk, I found a photograph of an object that belongs to me."

"Ah, now you've got my attention. I do believe that qualifies as a genuine mystery. And what were you doing going through his desk?"

"Looking for some kind of contacts to locate the man. Sheesh, you don't think I routinely snoop through people's private things?" She blushed, just a little. "Well, okay, I guess I do. It's part of my job."

"You don't have to defend it to me. I'm a big advocate of being informed. That's what you were doing, right? Looking for information."

Well . . . that might be stretching it a little bit. Sam squirmed in her seat. She'd never told Rupert about the powers of the wooden box, although he'd witnessed the results a couple of times.

"So, are you going back?" His surgically unlined face looked eager.

"I don't know."

His expression drooped.

"Well, eventually, I'll have to. The Montague place is still under my care."

"Montague? It wouldn't be *Will* Montague?"

Of course. Rupert would know William Montague if the man were wealthy and involved with the elites whose names Sam had spotted in his address book. She nodded.

"Oh, this explains a lot," Rupert said. "Will is one of the premier supporters of the arts here in Taos. He's not attended a single opening or gallery reception in absolutely *ages*. Very unlike him. *Very* odd."

"You don't happen to know if he's got relatives, do you—where they might be? The USDA is trying to make contact with someone who might handle his business, to see if they can get him up to date on the mortgage before they have to foreclose."

Rupert took a long sip of his tea, contemplating. "Off hand, I can't say. But let me give it some thought." He set the cup down. "It would be a colossal shame for the place to go up for auction—oh, Sam, is that what would happen?"

She shrugged. "I don't know for sure. Different procedures, I think, depending on the circumstances."

"Could I go with you? Out to his house? Oh, please, Sam. I've never been there but the man's art collection is legendary. I'd give anything just to gaze, to admire . . ."

"Art collection?" Sam searched her mental pictures of the house to remember the artworks. There'd been a lot of paintings, quite a few figurines and pieces that she'd thought of as knick-knacks.

If they were actually valuable art, she really ought to photograph the place and inventory the contents, in case there were any questions as the foreclosure proceeded. She'd never been assigned to a house where there was anything of true value, but she had a sneaking suspicion that she might be held responsible. Yikes. This could suddenly get sticky.

Rupert was staring and Sam realized that her face must have gone pale.

"You okay, sweetie?" he asked.

"Uh, yeah. Just thinking about all those valuable things out there. I guess I really should go back today." Her one day off and here she was, giving it away. "I could use your help."

Two people taking photos and writing descriptions—the work would move along that much faster. And Rupert's expertise would certainly be handy.

"I'm ready now," he said. "I wouldn't have gotten that lady out of the tower this morning anyway."

Sam smiled at his enthusiasm but gestured to her attire. A nightshirt and robe weren't exactly the right garb. "Let me get dressed. What time is it anyway?"

He tipped his wrist to get a look at the gold Rolex there. "Quarter past five."

"There's no electricity in that house," she said. "We at least have to wait until daylight. You can hang around here or I can get dressed and pick you up on my way. If you're up for a New Mexican breakfast we could stop at the Taoseño on the way?"

She knew he couldn't resist the breakfast burritos at the popular local restaurant.

"Pick me up at six-thirty." His voice sounded eager and his eyes sparkled. "I might even have my final chapter plotted by the time you get there." He reached for the purple greatcoat that he'd shed when he arrived and swooped out the door in customary Rupert fashion.

Chapter 10

S am cleared the tea tray and put the used cups into the
dishwasher as quietly as possible. No sense in disturbing
Kelly's one morning of rest. She left a note on the table and
made sure that she stuck the photograph and address book
into her backpack, along with her digital camera and a legal
pad.

Promptly on time, she pulled up at Rupert's house. He'd
dressed down slightly for their sleuthing operation—soft
gray knit pants and a blousy purple wool tunic, under a gray
hip-length down jacket.

"Good thing you put on warm clothes," she said.
"There's no heat out there, either."

The sun crested Taos Mountain as they came out of
the restaurant, and the sleepy town was beginning to show

signs of movement. Sam headed south along the main drag, Paseo del Pueblo Sur, and made the turns eastward to the now-familiar lane. Rupert's eyes focused on the house as Sam slowed to a stop.

"Maybe I should take his mail inside," she commented as they got out of the truck. "Hopefully, he wouldn't mind. It's already pretty evident that I've broken in."

Rupert clearly itched to flip through the mail to see what the wealthy man might have received, but Sam kept the stack neatly tucked under her arm while she worked the key in the back door lock.

The greatroom with its leather sofas and chairs and large fireplace, looked just as she'd left it, except that the early morning sun came through the windows from the opposite direction. Rupert immediately began to admire a pair of bronzes—cowboys on horses. He named the sculptor but Sam wasn't familiar with the work.

She set the mail on the granite counter and sniffed at the air in the kitchen. Stale, but the bad-food reek had subsided. She pulled the camera and writing pad from her backpack.

"How about if I snap pictures and you write descriptions, since you actually know what you're looking at," she suggested.

They went around the room, focusing on paintings and sculpture. Sam realized how little she knew about this whole world of high-dollar collectibles when Rupert pointed out an antique fire-screen and tools that he swore were pre-Civil War.

In the dining area Sam recognized an RC Gorman oil, which Rupert immediately spotted as an original and noted on the inventory with a value upwards of $50,000. Once again, Sam got an uneasy feeling. Nobody walked away from assets like these.

They worked their way through the rooms, even going so far as to photograph the kitchen appliances. In the library, Sam snapped wide angle shots of the bookcases, doing close-ups only when Rupert pointed out a section that he swore were first editions.

Sam felt her energy flagging. They'd been at it for three hours already and she felt chilled to the bone in the unheated house. The thought occurred to her that she might be able to make a pretty good case for having the power restored, just on the basis of the value of the art. Something might become damaged by the cold. But she wasn't sure how far Delbert Crow's authority went. A stronger argument might actually be made with Montague's insurance company, which could potentially be out hundreds of thousands in damage claims. She mused aloud about this to Rupert.

"Why don't you take the camera and the list and check both guest rooms and baths," she said. "I'll go through some of these files and see if I can get a name for his insurance agent."

He trooped out of the library and Sam took the leather chair at the desk once more. Before she touched it she realized that something was different. A stapler and metal ruler that had been in the top drawer yesterday now sat on top of the desk. A different kind of chill went through her already-cold arms.

She visualized the desk as she'd left it. Each item that she'd touched she'd replaced exactly in its spot. The center drawer was open a little less than an inch. It, too, showed signs of a search. The place where the address book had lain was no longer a blank spot—a scattering of index cards and paperclips covered it. She reached toward the back of the drawer to see what else might have been moved.

"Sam, I—" Rupert peeked into the room.

Startled, she jerked.

A faint whirring sound came from her left. Rupert stopped in mid-step and as Sam followed his gaze she saw that one section of the bookcase was slowly swinging outward.

"What the—" Her breath caught.

A dark void appeared behind the wooden case, which stopped at a ninety-degree angle to its normal position.

"Holy cr—" Rupert cleared his throat. "Girl, what have you done?"

Holy crap was right. Sam's vocabulary wasn't nearly as restrained as Rupert's and she filled in with a few other choice phrases as well.

"I . . . I don't know."

His eyes were as wide as hers felt.

"Do you still have that big flashlight, Sam? Cause I'm not standing here without—"

"Light. Good idea."

"No, I meant a weapon." His lips had gone pale.

"I left my backpack in the kitchen."

"I'll get it." He scurried from the room like a jittery rabbit. Sam rose from the chair and edged herself away from the black hole.

"Here," he breathed, so close that Sam jumped again. He handed her the light. *Thanks a lot, big brave guy.*

She snapped it on and aimed the bright LED beam toward the exposed space behind the bookcase. The cavernous space was at least eight feet deep. The light glinted off various surfaces—wood and glass.

"It's a whole room," Rupert whispered, standing two inches from Sam's shoulder.

She stepped closer and he trailed, like a second skin.

At the doorway, Sam stopped. The beam traveled past shelves and display cases, obviously custom built to fit the safe room. They appeared to be filled with small objects: a set of short bones, like a very small finger; metal implements, including a huge syringe, in a wooden box with fitted compartments for each item; another compartmented box that contained teeth, perfectly preserved molars with gold fillings and crowns. Atop one of the display cases sat a shaded lamp. Sam gasped when she realized that the base of it was made from a human skull. She flicked the light away from it, then back, then away again as a queasy feeling crawled into the pit of her stomach.

"Sam . . . I don't like this."

"Creepy. Looks like the guy's taste in collectibles goes a tad beyond paintings and Western sculpture."

She ran the beam along another display, this one filled with heavy-duty pliers and saws. A vision popped into her head, of a battlefield medical tent, an officer in bloodied whites amputating a leg. She blinked hard and the picture went away.

Her light bounced off the opposite wall of the confined space and landed on a dark figure, standing in the far left corner. Sam shrieked and bumped into Rupert as she jerked backward, her heart pounding.

"What? What is it?" Rupert said.

Her feet kept scrambling backward, her butt bumping him awkwardly.

She edged a glance over her shoulder and realized that

she'd backed him entirely out of the hidden room. She aimed the light back at the dark figure in the corner and assured herself that it wasn't a real person standing there. The hairs on her arms rose.

A Klansman, was her first thought. The floor length robe, the pointed cap that covered the face. But the material was a dark green, almost like military khaki but with a more yellowish cast, a sickly, ominous shade. Dark stains ran down the front of the robe. Whatever held it up—mannequin, dress form, or skeleton—placed the arms together at the waist, and out of the bell-like sleeves unseen hands held a tattered rope noose. In the mask, the eye holes were crudely cut, as if a vicious animal had gnawed them out. The holes were deep, empty and utterly black but Sam had the sickening feeling that they could somehow see her.

Chapter 11

Sam felt her scalp prickle and her entire body contract with goosebumps. Acid rose in her throat. She scrambled backward to get out of the doorway, surprised to find that Rupert was already halfway across the library, the other side of the massive desk. His eyes were about the size of dinner plates and Sam imagined that her own looked the same. Her breath was coming in gasps by the time she reached his side.

"What the hell—?"

"I don't know, but I'm not sticking around to find out," Rupert panted. He headed for the doorway.

"Wait. We can't just leave the room this way." C'mon, she thought, they were just *things*, inanimate objects. Creepy inanimate objects, but she'd dealt with a lot of disgusting things in this job. "Let me at least straighten up."

She took a deep breath and sidled around the edge of the desk. Sneaking up on the open bookcase, she pressed against it and was relieved when it swung soundlessly closed on its sturdy hinges. She heard Rupert give a nervous chuckle and saw that he stood in the door to the hall, watching her.

She jammed her hands to her hips. "Thanks a lot, mister bravado."

He looked a little sheepish.

"I'll just tidy the desk," she said, "and then let's get out of here." Beyond that, she had no idea what to do about the find. Her first thought was to report it to Beau, but although Montague's collection was weird, eerie, macabre, just about any creeped-out adjective she could think of . . . was it illegal? Probably not.

She gathered the few items that she'd removed from the drawer and jammed them back inside. She swiped the sleeve of her sweatshirt across the surface in a half-hearted attempt to remove the skiff of dust, then joined Rupert in the hall outside the library.

"Okay, let's go," she said, heading toward the kitchen. "You have my camera and our inventory list?"

Miraculously, the camera still hung from his wrist by its strap.

"Oh, Sam. I almost completely forgot. The reason I came looking for you in the library was because I found something." He was walking down the hall in the opposite direction. "I think there's been a break-in."

She turned around and trotted along behind him. When she caught up, in the front foyer, he was poised dramatically, one hand pointed at the heavily carved front door. A crack of light at the door's edge evidenced that it had, indeed, been compromised. Sam knew, from her first visit here, that this door was securely locked three days ago.

"Did you touch it at all?" she asked.

"Definitely not." He drew himself up even straighter. "I've written enough police procedure in my novels to know better than that."

Sam placed a fingertip high on the open edge and pulled it gently inward. No evidence that the lock had been picked or damaged. But that might not mean much. She, herself, could pick a lock with a simple set of tools, and there were even more sophisticated lock picks available. Then, too, it was simply possible that the intruder had a key.

This was all getting too complex for Sam to figure out on her own. The open door gave her the perfect reason to hand it all over to Beau and let the authorities deal with the situation.

She dipped her frozen fingers into her coat pocket and came out with her cell phone. He answered on the third ring.

"Hey there," he said, "enjoying your Sunday off?"

"Yeah, well, it's not exactly working out that way." She quickly explained how the decision to inventory the home's valuable contents had turned into the discovery of the open door, minus a mention of the hidden room and its unnerving contents—that could wait until he got here. "There were a few things out of place in the library, but otherwise I can't tell that anything is missing. But I thought I better report the break-in."

"I can't get out there now," Beau said. "In fact, it won't be for several hours. I don't even have a deputy I can send at the moment. We're up to our necks in calls for some reason today."

Sam didn't relish the idea of hanging around the

Montague house another ten minutes, let alone several hours.

"If the door isn't damaged, why don't you just lock it up again, make sure everything is secure. I can call you when I'm ready and you can meet me there, if that works for you."

Although Sam wasn't crazy about coming back out here once she settled in at home, she agreed. There certainly was no point in staying in the unheated house staring at an open door. And although Beau could surely just write up a report with the information she'd already given, there were a few other things she'd like for him to see. Taking care not to leave prints, she pushed the door closed and twisted the deadbolt.

Rupert helped her check the other entrances and windows and seemed more than relieved to leave the place behind as they gathered their inventory list and Sam's backpack. He offered to take her to lunch, but she begged off, saying that she really needed to get things done at home with the rest of her free day. She dropped him off at his place, leaving him with a stern warning not to blab all over town the fact that a valuable art collection was sitting unattended. Some among Rupert's artsy friends would give their eye teeth for those pieces.

Home at last, Sam found a note from Kelly stating that she'd made plans with a couple of old school buddies— dinner and a movie. It felt good to know she had the house to herself for awhile. The thought ran through her head— not for the first time—that it would be good for Kelly to get her own place. Even though she'd wrecked her credit rating with an overextended mortgage and maxed-out cards, she shouldn't be living at home with mom at this stage of her life.

The problem was that she needed to build up her savings so she wouldn't get into those same traps again, and now that her job as caregiver to Beau's mother was on hold for awhile, who knew what the future would bring. Sam didn't know what to suggest so she opted to run the bathtub full of very hot water and bath oil and soak away the cold that didn't want to leave her bones.

An hour later she'd bundled herself into her fluffy robe, made a chicken sandwich that would serve as both lunch and dinner, and settled into her favorite corner of the sofa with that book she'd been intending to read for a month. Unfortunately, her mind wouldn't stay focused on the storyline. Although they'd pretended to be brave at the time, the Klan-like robe with the dead eyes kept coming back to her. What kind of sinister collection was that, with the old medical tools, the teeth, the bones? It was obviously strange enough even to Montague that he kept it out of sight.

What if—the thought leapt at her—what if the photo she'd found of her wooden box were somehow tied with the other macabre items? Again, she had the thought that perhaps Bertha Martinez had been the target of some kind of plot, that she'd insisted on Sam taking the box so someone else couldn't get hold of it. The whole idea set her on edge.

She got up and carried her half-finished sandwich to the kitchen, dumping it into the trash, her appetite gone. Sitting quietly and attempting to read a book clearly wasn't happening either. She needed to be taking action.

Sam retrieved her backpack from the corner of the kitchen counter where she'd left it and pulled the camera and legal pad from it. She could download the photos to a disk to give to Beau. In addition to evidence of the open front door, he might need an official record of the home's contents, if it should turn out that someone were to claim that anything was missing.

As she sat at her desk, watching the little dots flow across the screen to indicate the progress of the download, her thoughts traveled to William Montague. What had happened to him? The more time she spent at his house, the more convinced she became that the man didn't simply abandon the place. He was nothing like the typical mortgage defaulter. He could have simply sold one or two pieces of art, if finances were the problem.

Plus, what about the other oddities? The broken vase in the bedroom, the fact that someone had come in within the past few days—seemingly taking none of the valuables, and yet leaving the front door ajar? Someone other than Sam had gone through the desk. For what? Had they taken something—the one item for which they'd come? It was certainly possible.

The camera gave a tiny musical tone, indicating that all the pictures had been saved. Sam glanced at the thumbnail-sized images in the folder, making sure she highlighted the correct ones before copying them to a disk for Beau. Toward the end of the sequence of shots, she spotted one in the library. It showed the bookcase-door swung open to the hidden room.

The image was skewed awkwardly; most likely Rupert had accidentally hit the shutter button at the moment he'd walked in. After that, they'd both been too astounded to even consider taking pictures. Well, it was probably a good thing that she include it with the photos for Beau. She intended to tell him about the room anyway. She hadn't decided, though, whether to bring up the connection to the box she possessed.

She didn't realize how far gone the day was when Beau finally called. She'd switched on a lamp at her desk and now it was the only pool of light in the house.

"Sorry, darlin', I really meant to get back to you sooner than this," he said.

"It's okay. I needed the chance to warm up. I've got the pictures for you."

"If you got the place secured all right, I don't see much point in going out there tonight. Without lights, we won't be able to get any more information than you collected today."

"True. It's not like there's a dead body on the premises or anything." The minute she said it, she shivered. Nothing like foretelling doom.

He didn't seem to notice. "I just finished my last call, and I really need to run by the hospital and see Mama. I could bring by some dinner afterward, as long as I don't get another call in the meantime."

"That's okay. I don't have much appetite at the moment." She realized that he probably just wanted to spend a little time with her. "I do, however, have the house all to myself."

"Maybe I better come there first. I can get out to the hospital anytime before nine tonight. And your place is right on the way . . ." He gave a little verbal leer and they hung up.

Normally, they would want more, but tonight quick sex might be just the thing. As she closed out the file of photos, remembering the frigid house and its disturbing contents, she knew that Beau's warm arms were exactly what she needed right now.

By the time his tap came at the door, she'd swapped the flannels and fuzzy robe for a slinkier gown and delicate slippers. He'd come straight from work but that didn't matter. She reached for his tie and pulled him into the room. His lips brought the winter evening inside, cool and warm at the same time. The second kiss melted away the outdoor chill and by the third kiss they began shedding clothing. His coat, Stetson and tie got lost somewhere along the way to the bedroom.

Later, snuggled into the curve of his arm, running her fingertip across his collarbone, she sighed.

Beau stretched and kissed the top of her head. "I better get going, much as I'd like to stay right in this very spot all night."

"I know. Me too."

As he dressed, she remembered to tell him that she'd made the inventory of the Montague place.

"I started to go through an address book that I found in the desk," she told him. "But I didn't find any quick or easy answers there. And I meant to look for the name of his insurance carrier. They might spring for the cost of having the power turned back on, just to avoid damage to some of his expensive things."

She pulled on her robe and went to her desk in the living room. "Here are the disk with all the photos, the address book, and this is the inventory list Rupert helped me with. I was lucky that he knew the names of a lot of the artists and had some idea of the value of some of the bigger pieces."

Beau took the items and set them on her kitchen table while he shrugged into his coat.

"Beau, there was something else out there. I don't quite know how to explain it. It was just plain weird."

"Can I ask you to come out there with me tomorrow? Maybe you can show it to me. I've also been thinking that I better bring a lab tech and just check the place carefully for evidence. With what you've told me, I'm thinking we better investigate this a little further."

They made tentative plans to meet up sometime around mid-morning, after Sam got the bakery open and made sure things were going well there. He gave her a lingering kiss and she felt again the wish that life could be less complicated.

Chapter 12

A pair of eyes stared at her from the depths of a hood. Black, fathomless, against the sickly green fabric. She wanted to turn and run but her muscles were frozen, rigid. A skeletal hand reached toward her throat.

Sam woke up, panting. Her arms and legs felt cold and stiff. She lay unmoving, not quite sure that it was only a dream. Gradually, her brain sent signals to her inflexible limbs, willing them to move. She stretched and sat up in bed, rubbing at her eyes. The clock told her that it was almost time to start her day. She clicked the alarm button off and sat on the edge of the bed, the dark images still too vivid.

Switching on the lamp dispelled most of the apparition. Too much visual input yesterday, she told herself. She forced her thoughts toward the morning and her duties at the bakery.

Gustav Bobul was standing at the alley door when Sam pulled up in her van. Huddled into his huge coat, he resembled a buffalo hunkered against the weather.

"You don't have to get here so early," she said. "I'm sure you're warmer at home. Just plan to come after six."

His puzzled expression made her wonder if she'd overcomplicated the way she phrased the idea. Or maybe he didn't really have a warmer home. Because of their unorthodox employment arrangement, he'd avoided giving her an address. She decided to leave it alone for now.

Before the ovens were preheated, Becky showed up and Sam handed over the calculations she'd made for creating large batches of Zoë's grandmother's recipes.

"As soon as the standard breakfast pastries are out, I'd like to get started with the cutouts," Sam suggested. "The dough may need refrigeration. I'm not sure how soft it's going to be. Once you can roll it, use these." She pointed out the special Star of David, oil lamp, and dreidl-shaped cookie cutters she'd bought. "I found a few pictures of the way they are traditionally decorated, with Hebrew letters on them. Think you can copy those?"

"Sure, no problem," Becky said after studying the pictures for a minute.

"And, we'll want macaroons."

Bobul piped up. "Bobul create a dark chocolate for to dip."

Sam nodded thoughtfully. "Sure, that would be great. Some of the macaroons can be plain, some with chocolate."

The recipe Sam was most eager to try was the rugelach and she started gathering flour, butter, cream cheese and the other ingredients. This one definitely needed to be chilled before rolling out and forming the crescent shaped cones that would be filled with cinnamon, sugar and raisins. She'd also decided to get creative and make a variety of jam fillings for a second batch. Before long, she was lost in the work.

When Jen and Kelly arrived at seven to open the store, the three in the kitchen looked up in surprise.

Bobul had already come up with some intricately formed wisps of garland for a two-foot-tall, all-chocolate Christmas tree he'd molded on Saturday. Sitting to one side were tiny candles and doves of white chocolate. Sam caught herself sneaking sidelong glances, amazed at the details the chocolatier kept adding.

Becky's first pans of muffins and coffee cakes came out of the ovens just as Jen asked for them. Cream puffs were already waiting on the cooling racks. The smell of coffee wafted back from the store, and Sam heard the tinkle of the bell at the front door.

"Customers—" Kelly stage-whispered through the doorway.

Jen walked out with two trays of muffins held high, and the day was off to its start.

Sometime between placing the rugelach dough into the fridge and making decorations for a sheet cake for the Chamber of Commerce's monthly dinner, Sam realized that Beau had walked in.

He glanced curiously at the hulking chocolatier in the corner but Sam distracted him. "I'll be ready to go in about ten minutes," she said. "Have Kelly get you some coffee and a scone or something."

He patted at his belly. "I'll pass on the breakfast. Had some eggs already. But the coffee sure does smell good."

He returned from the sales room with a mug in hand

and stood beside Sam's work table, watching her. "That's amazing, darlin', how you take that big floppy bag and out comes a flower."

She piped four poinsettias onto her waxed-paper topped flower nail, slid each one onto a baking sheet, and carried them to the fridge to firm up. The theme for the cake was Taos at Christmas, so it would be shaped like the plaza, with adobe buildings ringing the four sides of the square, each accurately depicting the actual businesses. In the center, she'd created a large Christmas tree by trimming round cake layers into a cone. The basic form was done, "dirty iced" with a preliminary coat of frosting, and cooling. In the morning she and Becky would add details, including the poinsettias which would decorate the four corners of the base, and then she would deliver it in the afternoon.

Climbing into Beau's department cruiser, Sam found herself working to mentally shift gears from baking to potential crime scene. This was the point where she really needed to share some things with Beau that she'd not told him last night.

She pulled the photo of the wooden box from her backpack. "Recognize this?"

His eyebrows drew together. "I've seen it. Where?"

"My house. I showed it to you awhile back. Remember Bertha Martinez? She gave the box to me right before she died."

"Oh yeah." He started the engine and backed out of his parking space.

"The photo was in Montague's house."

"That's odd." Beau eased into traffic. "Do you think they knew each other?"

"No idea. Her name wasn't in his address book. I

checked."

At the next light he made a right turn, heading down the main road through town.

"There's something else I'll show you when we get to his house. A collection of sorts. I'm not sure what else to call it. But it's a lot of weird stuff. I think maybe . . . I don't know . . . maybe he was after the box."

"To add to the collection?"

She shrugged. "You'll have to see this stuff to believe it."

Another vehicle sat in front of the Montague house when they drove up. The crime scene technician whom Sam had met before, Lisa, stepped out as Beau brought his white SUV to a stop.

"Okay, Sam, show us around," he said.

The icy patches from four days ago were now confined to the shady places in the yard, the bases of trees, the edges of the yard beside walls, crusty and littered with dirt and plant debris which had blown in. Sam led the way, showing Beau and Lisa the locked front door, then taking them around to the back where her key worked in the door to the central room.

"The place is gloomy and cold," she said as she signed the log-in sheet that the USDA required at each of her properties, "but I can show you the things I've noticed that seem out of place."

She took them to the master bedroom first, pointing out where she'd found the shattered glass vase near the bed, the strewn covers, and the condition of the adjoining bathroom. They took a peek at the shards she had placed in the wastebasket.

"It isn't much, Sam," Beau said. "Montague himself

may have just been in a hurry to leave. Dropped the vase and didn't bother to clean up."

"I know. I thought that at first, too. It's not that there's a great big clue here, it's more like a dozen little ones. Remember, there was also a big supply of food in the refrigerator, and a partially eaten meal left on the kitchen counter. It didn't feel like a place where the owner has left on vacation."

Lisa began to spray Luminol around the area where the glass shards had lain. Immediately, a large patch on the Persian rug glowed bluish.

"Blood," the tech said. "Quite a bit."

Beau knelt down and studied it. "Not enough that someone bled out. But it's definitely more than a nosebleed or your normal household cut."

"Look at this," Lisa said. She pointed into the trash. "The glass shards don't have any blood on them."

"Better bag up the glass and the rug," Beau said.

Lisa did so, then continued to work her way around the side of the bed.

"Bedding has some." She pointed out that the deep burgundy spread had both smears and droplets.

Amazing what isn't visible to the eye, especially in poor light, Sam thought. She wandered toward the closet and opened the door. The walk-in space was filled with clothing.

"Do you have a flashlight, Beau?"

He brought one over and aimed it into the dark space. "Two big suitcases, both look like they're sitting where they belong. No empty hangers, no gaps."

"It really doesn't look like he packed for a trip, does it?"

"We can't rule it out. He could own more bags, more clothes than what we're seeing here."

"But—"

"I'm not saying something hasn't happened here. The blood and the unfinished meal aren't normal findings. It's worth asking around, checking with neighbors and friends."

Lisa had come upon more blood drops near the French doors and Beau told her to get samples of that, as well.

Somewhat relieved, Sam took him around and pointed out the artwork that Rupert had identified as being fairly valuable. They ended up at the front door, where Beau instructed Lisa to dust for prints.

"The desk would be another place you might find prints," Sam said, reminding him that she'd found items out of place there too.

Lisa performed the duties, taking prints from the places Sam pointed out, along with a few where it was likely that no one but Montague might have left any. "To help us separate his from an intruder's," Beau said. "Considering that a man of his standing probably isn't in the system with a criminal record."

They would also discover Sam's. She'd been printed a few months ago, for the same reason, to eliminate her prints from others at a crime scene house.

Beau dismissed Lisa, suggesting that she get back to the office and process as much as she could. The blood swabs would need to go to the state crime lab in Santa Fe.

After the lab tech had left, Beau turned to Sam. "Okay, now I need to see that part you really don't want to talk about."

Chapter 13

Sam sighed and took him back to the library. At Montague's desk, she opened the center drawer and began feeling around inside.

"I don't know exactly how I triggered—" The low sound of the whirring gears interrupted. She tilted her head toward the moveable section of bookcase, which was swinging slowly outward.

Beau watched silently. When the dark opening was fully revealed, he let out a breath. "Well, look at that. A real secret room."

"Wait 'til you see." Sam reached for the flashlight he still carried and aimed it into the cavern.

Everything looked the same as the day before—the antique wooden display cases with their contents of bizarre medical implements, the tiny child-sized bones, the lamp with the skull base, and the eerily heart-stopping sight of the dark figure in hate-garb.

"What the hell is *that*?" Beau said, recoiling from the sight.

"I don't know. I had the same reaction." She still did, Sam realized as she bumped the edge of the doorway behind her.

She handed the flashlight to Beau and turned away from the hidden room and those hollow eyes. Last night's dream rushed back at her.

Beau stepped into the void and she could see the beam of light as it circled the space. When he stepped out, his expression was tight.

"That is just too weird for words," he said.

"Well, at least it's too weird for me. I guess people get into collections of all types of things." She thought of one of her more recent properties, where a young woman had hoarded everything from newspapers to baby clothes.

"You said this had something to do with that wooden box?" Beau switched off the flashlight.

"I don't know," Sam said. "I found that photo of the box in the desk, during my first inspection of the house. I'm sure it's my box because the picture was taken in the back bedroom at Bertha Martinez's house. Remember it? The one with the red walls and all the witchy symbols?"

He nodded and stared again at the photo, which Sam had pulled out of her coat pocket. After about a minute he silently handed it back to her. "Watch yourself," he said. "I don't know why, exactly, but I have a gut feeling about this."

She tucked the picture back into her pocket.

"I think I'll spend a little time talking to Montague's neighbors. You probably don't want to hang around for that. Maybe I can buy you lunch and then get you back to work?"

As she closed the desk drawer, after they'd pushed the bookcase back in place, Sam remembered that one of the main reasons she'd wanted to come back to the house was to get the name of Montague's insurance company. She flipped through files until she came to a copy of the billing. She pulled the page out and folded it.

They rechecked all the doors and walked out into the chill sunshine of the December day. The sky was brilliant blue, so bright that it hurt to look.

"What about getting the power turned on in the house?" Sam asked as they pulled up at Beau's favorite burger place. "I'll call the insurance agent, if you'd like."

He nodded, but his real concentration became diverted by placing his order for a burger loaded with cheese and green chile.

* * *

Back at Sweet's Sweets, Sam found things in a state of semi-chaos. The school nurse had called and Becky had dashed out to take her youngest home with a sore throat. Four sheets of macaroons were in the oven and Kelly was doing her best to guess at whether they were done. Sam took a peek and told her to give them exactly two more minutes, then pull them out and get them onto cooling racks.

In the sales area, Jen had her hands full with demands for cheesecake—they were running low on Sam's special amaretto and things were getting a little ugly out there. Sam ran referee and convinced one customer that the pecan praline was every bit as good, averting a purse-swinging battle between two women who were normally quiet little churchgoers. She'd no sooner gotten them settled at tables with their desserts and coffee than a harried man roared to a stop in his Corvette and dashed inside, his eyes roaming the displays frantically.

Wife's birthday, forgot a cake. Sam could spot 'em a mile away.

She walked over to him before he got the chance to unleash on Jen for the lack of decorated cakes in the displays.

"I've got something very exclusive that I haven't brought out yet," she said. "My chief decorator is just finishing it up. If you'll have a complimentary cup of coffee and give me ten minutes?"

The word 'exclusive' stopped him in his tracks. Sam pointed him toward the coffee setup.

Becky had baked layers this morning and Sam hustled to the fridge and surveyed the choices. Chocolate or vanilla. A man this nervous has a wife who's going to bite his head off, and the reason she would do that is because she's smack in the middle of PMS. Definitely chocolate to fix that.

Sam grabbed up two of the chocolate layers and a pot of fudge filling. Splitting the layers she filled them to create a four-layer torte, frosted the sides and top with ganache, and pressed slivered almonds to the sides. A shell border of chocolate buttercream, some shavings of white chocolate . . . she held up the finished piece. It was lovely, if she did say so herself.

The man looked up from the display case, where he was choosing a dozen cookies, and his face lit up.

"You saved my bacon," he said under his breath, as he pulled cash from a clip.

"Happy to do it," Sam told him.

Jen placed the torte into one of their purple boxes and tied a gold ribbon around it. "There," she said brightly. "All nice and pretty."

Sam and Jen exchanged a glance as the man headed for his car. "I don't know whether to hope he tells everyone that he got such great service here, or not. We might find ourselves solving ten of these crises a day."

"We can handle it," Jen said.

Sam was in the middle of taking a quick mental inventory of the displays when a middle-aged woman with short blond hair came in.

"I need another of those little boxes," she said, glancing around at the displays, not seeing what she wanted.

Sam pointed out the boxed chocolate assortments.

"No, not like those," the woman said. She ran her fingers through her inch-long blond layers. "This was about like so . . ." she said, indicating the size of a playing card. "The whole box was made of chocolate and it had tiny gold jewelry inside."

"We've never had—" Jen started to say.

Sam piped up. "I know the piece you mean. It was made as a sample, one of a kind, and we don't have any more." She steered the lady toward a quiet corner.

"But—" The woman seemed near tears. "I—I—"

What was going on here?

Sam grabbed a cup from the coffee bar and filled it with water. "Did something happen with that chocolate box?" she asked in a low voice.

The lady took a long sip and looked around the room,

as if more copies of the box might have appeared. Luckily, Jen had gotten busy with another customer.

"I took the box home the other day. It was so cute that I didn't really want to eat it, but something just came over me and I had to take a taste. Then I had another taste. My daughter was there and she ate about half of it. Before I knew it, the whole thing was gone."

Sam smiled. "Our chocolates *are* good. I'm glad you liked it."

"That's not the thing. See, my daughter and her husband were having problems. She came over to tell me she was leaving him. I was so afraid that they would break up and leave the children with terrible memories of Christmas without their mother."

Sam tried to figure out where this story was going.

"Jake walked into the room just as we were finishing the chocolate. He and Christine took one look at each other and it was like it was their wedding day. They had such love in their eyes, they hugged, they kissed. They completely made up. They're back together, as if nothing bad ever happened."

Power of suggestion? Sam worked to keep her expression neutral. "That's wonderful news. I'm so happy to hear it."

"So now I need another one," the woman said.

"But the problem is fixed."

"Oh, the second box would be for my son. He's so lonely. He needs a girlfriend but the right one hasn't come along."

Oh boy. What if Sweet's Sweets became known as a rescue place for the lovelorn? Sam took a look at the woman's wistful expression. Oh, hell, what could it hurt? She took the lady's elbow and steered her toward the sales counter.

"All of our chocolates are made with the same ingredients. I'm sure you'll find these varieties will also be to your liking."

As the lady chose a box and pulled out money to pay for it, Sam almost stopped her. What if she didn't get the results she wanted? This was crazy. No chocolate box had saved someone's marriage. It was purely coincidence. This lady's family situation would turn out however it was meant to turn out.

The cash register dinged and Jen handed over the boxed chocolates. "Have a magical day," she said.

Sam sent her a look, as the customer walked out the door.

"What? I always say that," Jen said.

"Oh, nothing. It's fine." It better be fine, Sam thought as she wandered to the back, remembering that she still needed to call Montague's insurance company.

It took about thirty minutes to get the agent to understand who she was and why she cared about someone else's home. It wasn't until she glanced over the inventory list that she'd carried in her pack that morning and did the head-math to the tune of over a million dollars, that he got the idea that maybe it would be smart to have heat in the house. He agreed to work things out with the electric co-op and to get on it immediately.

Sam pushed back in her chair and took a breath.

Bobul continued to work his delicate magic with his chocolate. Racks of finished creams, truffles and molded holiday shapes sat all around him. Kelly was at work with plastic-gloved hands, choosing assortments and filling the boxes.

"We're nearly out of the first batches," Sam said. "Take these out front as you get them ready."

She got to her feet and checked out the condition of the rugelach dough she'd left in the fridge. Perfect. As she rolled it out and cut it into wedges she found herself wondering if Beau was learning anything from Montague's neighbors. Maybe they could chat tonight and catch up.

She smeared half of the small dough triangles with apricot jam and began rolling them up like little crescent rolls. The other triangles got a treatment of cinnamon and sugar, with a sprinkling of finely chopped walnuts. Once they went into the oven, Sam popped out to the sales area to see how things were going. Several of the gift-boxed chocolates were already gone and Jen was ringing up a sale for two more. Hiring Bobul was turning out to be one of her better business decisions.

Riki Davis-Jones, the next-door dog groomer, bustled in wearing her plastic apron over jeans and a bright red sweater. She dropped some bills on the counter and grabbed up the two boxes of chocolates.

"A customer told me about these. Sam, you've been keeping secrets . . ."

If she only knew.

"If I can get these out to the post today, they might still make it to me mum in time. She's a big fan of chocolate at Christmas." She seemed to belatedly remember the apron, and began pulling it off as she headed out the door.

She passed Rupert, who looked like a man with a purpose—a purple-clad man with a purpose—as he pushed his way into the store.

"Girl, I want to know why I had to hear it on the street that you've got a chocolate wizard in your shop now," he said, grabbing Sam in a hug before she had time to say hello.

"He's just been here a couple of days, Rupe. Sorry I forgot to mention it."

"So, let me in on the delectable secret. What's he making today?"

Sam held up the plate of samples and he promptly grabbed up one that featured a chocolate truffle base with a scattering of sugar snowflakes.

He actually whimpered as he let the first bite dissolve on his tongue. "Must have. Must have," he mumbled.

"This maple cream with the burnt sugar base is amazing too," Jen said, and Rupert immediately reached for a sample piece of that one as well.

"Oh my, yes." He eyed the boxes stacked near the register.

"These contain assortments." Jen raised the lid of one to reveal a dozen, each chocolate morsel elegantly decorated with winter and holiday motifs. "Or, we can make up full boxes of any flavor you would like."

Sam glanced toward the kitchen, hoping that Bobul and Kelly were keeping up.

Rupert's gaze went to the ceiling as he ticked off a checklist on his fingers. "I'll need seven boxes for tonight—opera guild gathering, you know. The assorted ones will be excellent."

Jen pulled the five remaining boxes aside and picked up the intercom to request that Kelly bring more.

"I really started out for a slice of your fabulous pumpkin cheesecake," he told Sam. "Join me?"

Traffic in the shop had slowed a bit, and Jen seemed to have everything under control. Kelly bustled through the doorway and set down ten more boxes of chocolates. Jen snagged the ones she needed to finish Rupert's order, and another customer immediately took one for herself. Sam raised an eyebrow toward Kelly, which was meant to convey *keep it coming!*

Rupert had poured two mugs of the Sweet's Sweets house-blend coffee and took a seat at one of the bistro tables, lighting up when Sam put his pumpkin cheesecake in front of him. She'd noticed a damaged blueberry muffin in the display case. Not perfect enough for a customer, she decided, so she'd taken it for herself. It felt good to simply sit down for a few minutes.

"Anything new with Will Montague's big mystery?" Rupert asked, once he'd polished off two hefty bites of his dessert.

Sam glanced around the shop. At least he'd waited to ask until there were no other customers.

"Beau is looking into it. Things don't look quite right there."

"I'll say. That horrid mask!"

"Rupe, you're not telling anyone else about this are you? I mean, please don't."

"Sam, I am the soul of discretion. Truly."

Yeah, but he was also a romance writer and a gossip, and who knew what stories might end up either in a book or as the latest tell-all at a dinner party.

"The man obviously wanted to keep that particular collection hidden away, privately. We have to respect that," she said, pulling bite-sized hunks off the muffin.

He squirmed a little. "I know. I won't say anything at all until I have the chance to clear it personally with Will."

Now Sam squirmed—she couldn't very well tell Rupert about the blood they'd found in Montague's bedroom. Or that there was a very good chance something awful had happened to his friend. He might not ever be coming back.

She covered by taking a long sip from her coffee.

"I know you and he hung out with the same group of art lovers," she said. "Has anyone said anything about where he might have gone?"

"Not a word. But I'll tell you who we might talk to. Bunny Fitzhugh. They say she and Will go *way* back. Rumor was that at one time—"

"Rupert—" Sam tilted her head toward the sales counter, where two new customers were perusing the displays. Rupert finished off his cheesecake while they made their selections and left.

"Maybe Ms Fitzhugh would know if Montague had travel plans," she said as he sipped the last of his coffee. "Do you think it would be possible for me to ask her a few questions?"

Rupert glanced at his Rolex, then pulled a phone from somewhere in the depths of the black and purple wool coat he'd draped over the back of his chair. He held the little instrument out at arm's length and squinted as he thumbed down a list.

When he started the conversation with "Bunny! Darling!" Sam got up to carry their cups and plates to the back. She lost track of the exchange as she scanned the kitchen to be sure everything was running smoothly. Her rugela were waiting in golden splendor on a cooling rack, Bobul hummed as he worked in his own little world, and Kelly had nearly finished boxing the finished chocolates.

Before she left, Becky had baked the fruitcake as

instructed, and a finished one now waited to be sampled. Sam cut a small slice and mulled the flavors around in her mouth. Plenty of nuts, fruit that was not at all bitter, and the dough melted in her mouth. A little adjustment to the spices, but this version was just about right.

"Bunny can see us at three," Rupert said, poking his head through the opening in the curtain.

Sam nodded, although she noticed that he'd already hung up the phone. Apparently, the meeting would take place on Bunny-time or not at all.

Chapter 14

Three o'clock was only twenty minutes away and Sam wasn't sure she would have time to change into something less sugar-dusted and still make it.

"Not to worry," Rupert said. "I told her that you are only *the* premier baker in all of Taos. She'd probably be disappointed if you *didn't* show up in your white jacket."

Sam grabbed a small fruit tart that Becky had made this morning, and placed it in one of her purple boxes. A little gift never hurt when it came to asking for dishy gossip from a stranger. They walked out to Rupert's Land Rover.

The big vehicle wound its way up a steep road on the east side of town, where the society divorcee (who "took the bastard to the cleaners," according to Rupert) lived in an adobe mansion that made the Montague place look positively tract-home. The sun was already midway down the western half of the sky, casting a pink-gold glow over the mountainside property and setting off the surrounding trees as if they were high-def. He parked and they stepped out into a bracing winter breeze.

Sam followed Rupert past a tall wooden gate with hardware that looked as if it came from some European dungeon. Inside the gated courtyard, two men were in the process of hanging strings of blue lights on four enormous blue spruce trees. A wreath the size of a kid's wading pool hung in a high archway above the front door.

"Nice digs," Sam mumbled.

"Bunny's little gift to herself after the divorce. She couldn't stand living in Dallas. She came to Taos on an art trip and fell in love. With this house." He lifted a brass knocker, which fell with a heavy *thunk*.

A tiny woman opened the door. Despite its size the massive door swung inward for her, smoothly and silently.

"Marietta, how are you dear?" Rupert asked.

The maid wore black slacks and a white shirt, not too unlike Sam's own bakery garb. She smiled shyly at Rupert and murmured a response with her head ducked. She stepped aside and Rupert breezed in, with Sam close behind.

"The sun room?" he asked.

Marietta nodded and indicated a door on their left. Rupert seemed to know the layout perfectly well, and Sam followed along as the maid withdrew silently.

The southern exposure and floor-to-ceiling windows gave the sunroom its apt name. Long beams of late-afternoon light crossed at a steep angle and landed on a black grand piano. White overstuffed sofas flanked a fireplace of dark river stone, with a charcoal gray rug providing a soft counterpoint to the black marble flooring. A lavish pot of white poinsettias sat on a coffee table.

Bunny herself provided the only spot of color in the monochrome room. Sam guessed her age at about thirty-five, as she rose from the white sofa. Her short orange hair fit her head like a cap, accentuating a sharp nose and strong jaw line. Her jumpsuit in shades of yellow and purple left the impression of a Cirque de Soleil performer—definitely someone who needed to be the most noticed item in the room.

Sam watched as Bunny and Rupert did a whole bunch of darling-this and darling-that before they turned toward her. In her own black and white work clothing, she felt more like an invisible servant than ever when she handed over the bakery boxed tart.

"Ah, Samantha, it's *so* good to meet you. I understand that you have the *most* adorable shop. I must get in there." Bunny lifted the lid of the box and breathed deeply. She dipped one of her French manicured fingers inside and came up with a small dollop of the filling. Sucking the creamy custard from her fingertip, she grinned like a naughty child. "Ooh, this *is* good!"

Sam smiled. Maybe the woman wasn't a complete snob.

"I'm doing a little holiday gathering here next weekend," Bunny said. "I do hope Pedro's men are getting the outdoor trees done . . ." She glanced around, as if that would make a difference. "Anyway, I would love to have one of your fabulous pastries as the centerpiece of the dessert table, dear."

"I'm sure we can come up with just the right thing," Sam said, making the mental shift from the real reason they'd come here. Her calendar was packed, with the two weddings and everything else, but how could she refuse the woman, right here in front of Rupert? Plus, she still wanted information.

"Seventy or eighty people, winter theme, not especially Christmas . . . we've got all persuasions here, you know."

"Cake? Torte? Maybe some smaller, assorted pastries?"

"Oh, a cake. I think that would be very special."

Sam began to envision possibilities.

"You'll be here, won't you, Rupert dear? It's the whole art crowd. I think a nephew of O'Keefe may even be able to make it—I do think you'll like him."

"Do you think William Montague might be coming?" Sam asked.

The momentary freeze on Bunny Fitzhugh's face would have been comical in a movie. Here, it might have marked Sam's social blunder of the season. Sam stared at Rupert. *Help me out here*, she telegraphed.

"Ah, yes," he piped up. "It's been ages since I've seen Will. I do hope you've been in touch with him."

"Will? Actually, it's been awhile." Bunny busied herself for a minute, calling for Marietta from the doorway, handing off the bakery box.

"Yes, but you two were quite the item for awhile, weren't you?" Rupert's teasing grin eased the tension and Bunny actually dimpled up.

"A lady never tells," she said, eyebrows arched.

"I was under the impression that he was continuing the courtship . . ."

Courtship? Did people really use words like that anymore? Sam turned away, occupying herself by looking at a collection of framed photos beside the fireplace.

Rupert kept his tone light, continued the teasing until Bunny was actually blushing.

"Oh, you know me too well, darling. But it was only a fun little flirtation. I was a married woman!"

More than a few marriages have broken up on that basis, Sam thought. She made a mental note to ask Rupert more about it later. The conversation between the two chums took a different direction and Sam chewed at her lip, trying to figure out how to get back to the topic of William Montague and whether he might have divulged any travel plans to his friends.

"Well, dears," Bunny said, after about ten minutes of inane chatter. "I'm afraid I must excuse myself. Dinner plans, you know. My bath, nails, hair . . ."

Sam couldn't see a single thing that could be improved upon. Two minutes to slip the jumpsuit off and get into a dress and shoes . . . But maybe that's why she never got invited to any glamorous parties, except as the baker to deliver the dessert.

Speaking of which, she reconfirmed the requirements and price for Bunny's holiday cake as they were subtly being ushered toward the front door.

"I'll have it here for you next Sunday," she promised.

Bunny gave a distracted nod, her mind obviously already elsewhere.

Aside from the cake order, that visit was certainly a waste of a good fruit tart, Sam thought as she climbed back into Rupert's vehicle. No real information about William

Montague, and now she'd loaded herself up with another job that she didn't really have time to do. She sighed.

Beside her, Rupert chuckled as he steered down the narrow lane leading into town. "I didn't believe that *married-woman* excuse for a second, did you?" he said. "Bunny was *so* unhappy with Larry Lissano. No one faulted her a bit for her 'little flirtations'. And no one was the least bit surprised when she and Larry split. Except maybe Larry."

"His name wasn't Fitzhugh?"

"Oh, heavens no. Bunny reverted back to her maiden name the very second they were divorced. Lissano was a name that only meant something to Larry's crowd, and believe me, Bunny didn't want to be associated with them any longer than she had to."

"Why was that?"

"Ah, I guess you never heard."

And why would I? But she didn't need to voice it. Rupert was well into another of his gossipy stories.

"Larry had tons of money, certainly. I mean, why else would Bunny have been attracted to him in the first place? As I heard it her grandparents were poor Irish in New York and her parents barely made it a step above that. She *never* admits this to anyone, but there's always somebody who can dig out the old garbage, you know? Well, Bonnie Fitzpatrick got a scholarship to Brown, dumped her family like a bunch of rotten potatoes, became Bunny Fitzhugh, and started hanging around with the Ivy League types.

"That group accepted her marginally. I mean, they knew she wasn't one of them. For her part, she used them as a finishing school. Learned how to speak well, do her hair, adopted the mannerisms." He'd reached the traffic light near the plaza and turned toward Sweet's Sweets.

"Along comes Larry Lissano. Rich. New money rich. The Ivy bunch would have nothing to do with him, but Bunny fell hard and fast. It happens to everybody who's never had much. Diamonds and jewelry, a fleet of fast cars, all the showy trappings. Bunny already had a clue that she wasn't going to bluff the East Coast bunch for very long. Moving to Dallas with Larry was a way to live the high life without having to explain her lack of pedigree."

"So, where did Larry get all this money? Win a lottery or something?"

"They *say*—and I don't know this for a fact—but the rather believable rumor was that his business dipped into a few slightly illegal trades."

"Drugs?"

Rupert shrugged. "I don't know . . . Like I said, it was all rumor."

"But Bunny didn't know this?"

"Or ignored it. She was purely in it for the money and the status money can buy. The home they built outside Dallas was over fifteen-thousand square feet and every square inch was a showplace. I visited there once, soon after I met her, and got lost in the guest wing. I had my own swimming pool, and three servants to fetch whatever I wanted."

Sam couldn't begin to imagine a life like that.

"I felt for her," Rupert said. "The gloss wore off the romance very soon, and all she had to do was to decorate, buy art, have lunch with a bunch of women who were in similar situations. The brain that got her into Brown University was far too wasted on that crowd. I was surprised that she stayed married to him for twelve years."

"So she decided to take what she could and get out?"

"Basically. Larry might have been a savvy businessman,

but he didn't give Bunny credit for the smarts to outmaneuver him financially. So, no pre-nup. When she got the most vicious divorce lawyer in Texas to represent her, well, Larry didn't stand a chance. She got enough to set her up for life, herself and every charity she might ever choose."

He parked behind the bakery and they sat in the Rover with the motor running.

"Bunny is a one-woman patron of the arts in this state, plus several other pet projects she has going on elsewhere. The divorce settlement was three years ago and she's begun doing a lot of good for a lot of people. "

"Do you think part of William Montague's art collection came from her generosity?"

"You know, I hadn't thought of that, but I wouldn't be surprised. I think he was Bunny's paramour, shall we say, at the time of the breakup. When she received her settlement check she went a little crazy. That house you just saw, all the furnishings . . . she spent like a wild woman. Not to mention the art she brought from the Dallas place. She knew good pieces, and she was smart enough to stipulate that part of her settlement would consist of certain artworks. Just the bit I know about art—Sam, I know she took at least a million in paintings and sculpture. Larry was a mad hornet, I'll tell you."

And revenge was . . . Sam pictured Larry Lissano easily harboring a grudge for three years.

"I'm surprised Bunny isn't afraid for her life. Surely if Larry has connections with dangerous people—"

"I know. I've wanted to caution her about being so visible."

Sam remembered the blood stain on William Montague's

bedding and a shiver ran through her. Bunny might not be the only target of revenge.

Chapter 15

S am watched Rupert maneuver the large SUV down the
alley and then walked back into her business. The kitchen
seemed quiet enough. Chocolate molds covered the work
table, waiting for whatever Bobul was patiently stirring at
the stove. He answered with a tilt of his head when Sam
asked how things were going.

Out front, Kelly and Jen were coping with the afternoon
dessert crowd. The coffee urns were about half full and the
pastry displays appropriately lean for this time of day. Sam
suggested to Kelly that she rearrange the remaining items
so there weren't obvious gaps. Jen gave Sam a subtle nod
and showed her the day's subtotal on the register. Not bad.

Sam issued a couple more orders to the girls and then
went to the back to write down Bunny Fitzhugh's instructions

for her winter party cake. Sam thought ice-blue fondant over a two-tier hexagon cake, with sugar snowflakes, some hand-piped bunting, and maybe a frosty white topper of some sort. She would have to give that some thought. She'd just finished sketching out her ideas when Beau appeared in the doorway from the sales area.

"Hey, beautiful," he said, sending his gorgeous grin her way.

Sam immediately looked down at her clothing, which was relatively free of flour smudges, for once.

"It's not what you're wearing," he reminded. "It's you."

She marveled again at whatever wonderful twist of fate had brought this kind and loving man into her life.

"How's your mom doing today?" she asked, feeling a stab of guilt that she'd not yet stopped by the hospital.

"Better. Every day is an improvement." He propped one hip on her desk. "Doc says she may go to the rehab facility next week or the week after."

"That's great news, Beau. I'm so happy to hear it."

"Well, it won't be the end of the problems. We'll have to figure out whether we can manage at home, even with Kelly's help. We may still be looking at a nursing home."

Hard news to handle, especially at the holidays, Sam thought.

"But that's not why I stopped by," he said. "I had a busy afternoon and thought I'd fill you in. Can you break away for coffee? A drink? Dinner?"

She chuckled. He always tried to be so accommodating, even though he was the one with the important job and more responsibilities.

"Whatever I can do dressed like this. Or I have to go

home and change." She tamped her bakery orders into a stack and set them in their basket. "I've got some interesting developments to tell you about too."

They agreed that drinks at one of their favorite small bars would be relaxing and probably the most private at this time of day. She walked Beau to the front door and suggested he grab them a quiet table at the back and she would be five minutes behind.

"Can you girls handle things until closing?" Sam asked, surveying the small crowd in the sales room.

"No problem," Kelly assured her.

By the time she walked into the little pub-style place just off the plaza, she found Beau at a corner table with a soda in front of him and a glass of red wine at the place beside him. A young guy was just setting a basket of tortilla chips on the table.

"Figured I better not have a drink," Beau said. "Technically, I'm on duty for another thirty minutes." He patted the radio at his hip. "At least it's been a quiet afternoon."

They reached for chips and dunked them in the bowl of red salsa that sat beside the basket.

"Okay, news? You first," Beau said.

Sam filled him in on the visit to Bunny Fitzhugh's lavish home and Rupert's later revelation that Bunny's ex-husband might very well have a motive to come after Will Montague.

"I don't know if the idea that Larry Lissano was a drug dealer or something is just rumor. But it could be true, and if so he could be a pretty dangerous man," she said.

Beau jotted the names in his small notebook. His expression was pensive as he said, "It's worth a look. Guy like that, even if he doesn't personally pull the trigger, he sure would have connections."

"Bunny claims that she hasn't had contact with Montague in 'ages.' I didn't get the chance to pin her down and ask exactly when she did last see him. I guess I could have done better at that."

"Don't worry about it. It looks like our investigation is going to ramp up. We'll probably have to question her again anyway."

"So, your news? Did you get the chance to ask around among Montague's neighbors?"

"A few. It's hard to canvass a neighborhood by yourself, in an afternoon, but I managed to find a few folks at home." He scooped up more salsa. "Unfortunately, the two on either side of his place really don't know him that well. One guy is a traveling salesman, rarely home. They've said hello out at the mailboxes a couple of times. The other is a stay-home mom, so she watches the neighborhood a bit more closely. But she didn't say much about Montague other than he drove a nice car but he didn't come and go much."

"That brings up a point," Sam said. "We never did check the garage, see if he had cars at the house or if any were missing. How would we know?"

"I did that. After I talked to the third neighbor, a guy right across the road. He told me that Montague worked from home. Some kind of internet business, buying and selling collectible art or antiques or something like that—his words. I didn't mention that we'd come across a few of the odder collectibles."

"Makes sense," she said. "Remember the printer sitting on the desk? No computer though. A guy can't run an internet business without a computer. So, someone has taken it. I first thought Montague, when we believed he'd just gone on a trip."

"Yeah. But I told you that I went ahead and checked the garage? Two spaces, two vehicles. There's a small convertible, a Honda S2000, parked with the top down as if he'd just come in from a summer drive."

"But this is December, so he hasn't touched that car in awhile. And that fits with the time-frame when he disappeared from the radar."

"Right. The other vehicle is an SUV, Cadillac Escalade. I'd guess that it hasn't been driven in months either. There's a fine layer of dust on everything in that garage, and there were no footprints near either vehicle. I'm having my office run the plates and VINs, just to see if anything turns up."

"Hmm. Sure doesn't tell us much." Sam sipped from her wine. "But it doesn't make sense that Montague left voluntarily. If he went on a trip he'd have packed a bag, taken clothes and toiletries, driven one of his cars to the airport. He'd certainly have made arrangements to pay his bills while he planned to be gone."

"I think that's key. I don't think he *planned* to be gone. I don't like the blood. I don't like the missing computer. Those would point to someone else having been there and taken Montague and his computer, against his will."

"But all that expensive art? That just doesn't make sense."

"Unless the crime was purely revenge, without robbery as a motive."

"So, now what?"

"We need to search the rest of the property. Behind that house are a lot of trees, heavy shrubbery. There could be a body out there. In this cold weather, a shallow grave . . ."

Sam shuddered.

"Meanwhile," Beau said, "I've got a deputy at work on the address book. We'll see if we can find anyone, friend or relative, who's heard from Montague. If no one is willing to file a missing person's report, the department will take over and conduct an investigation."

A tiny digital sound came from Beau's watch. "Well, I'm officially off duty now," he said. "Want to go ahead and make this dinner? I'll need to run by the hospital before I can go home, so this might be my chance to eat."

"Maybe I'll come along and visit Iris for a little while."

They ordered thick sandwiches from the bar menu and Sam pondered what she had learned about William Montague while she ate.

The more she thought about it, the less likely it seemed that the man was going to be found alive and well. And she really wished she'd gotten the chance to meet him and ask why on earth he had a photo of her jewelry box.

Chapter 16

Sam's cell phone rang as she reached her van. Beau stood by as she plucked it from her pocket.

"Hey, Kel. What's up?"

"Jen and I are ready to go home, but Bobul wants to stay awhile. He's cooking something that he says will get ruined if he doesn't finish tonight. At least I *think* that's what he was telling me." She lowered her voice a little. "Anyway, I didn't know if you'd want me to leave him alone here. I mean, I shouldn't give him a key or anything, should I?"

"Let him finish," Sam said. "I can come by before I go home." She would miss seeing Iris but she could use the time to do some preliminary prep for the morning and to make sure they were on top of tomorrow's orders while the chocolatier finished his tasks.

She explained and gave Beau a brief kiss, waving a quick goodbye as his department cruiser drove away.

When Sam arrived, Bobul was still at the stove, slowly stirring something that smelled like caramel. The work table was cleared of chocolate molds, and boxes of truffles sat in neat ranks at one side.

"The customers sure are crazy about your chocolates," she told him.

"Bobul chocolate no make insane," he said.

Something got lost in *that* translation. Sam laughed and tried to correct the misconception. "No, Bobul, I mean that they like them. They like them a lot."

Over his shoulder, he gave one of his little lopsided grins.

While he removed the caramel from the stove and started to do something with it, Sam mixed up enough of the dry ingredients for her standard breakfast pastries. She'd learned that by making up a couple of five-gallon buckets of dry mix each afternoon, she could sleep an extra few minutes in the morning. When she came in she could blend the eggs and milk, add the right amount of her premixed dry ingredients, and then adjust the spices, add fruit. It wasn't a huge time savings but on days that tended to get a little crazy, it helped.

She peeked in on the Chamber of Commerce cake-in-progress, noting the huge amount of work she and Becky would need to do to get it out the door by the following afternoon. Which reminded her that Becky had left midday with a sick child. She dialed her assistant's home while she pulled food coloring from the shelves. Becky sounded non-committal but there wasn't a lot Sam could say. She remembered what it had been like, having to work when your child occasionally got sick. But it sure couldn't have come at a worse time. Sam hung up with a groan. Maybe Kelly could learn some of the decorating techniques quickly.

Meanwhile, she did a quick inventory of staples and went to the computer to place an order. Once she'd clicked the Send button on her supply order, she had a thought.

Quickly entering William Montague's name in her search engine, she was surprised to see his name come up in five separate listings. Montague Art & Collectibles seemed to be his official business name. She clicked the link.

Fine art and rare collectible items for the discriminating collector.

Photos showed paintings—a couple of which Sam remembered seeing in his home—and ornate pieces of furniture. Interesting. Maybe nothing in Montague's house actually belonged to him; maybe the whole place consisted of inventory in his business.

Before she had the chance to ponder that, Bobul announced that he was ready to leave. Sam saw that it was after eight o'clock and she felt her own energy lagging. She shut down the computer.

"Bobul, how do you get home?" she asked. She'd never seen a vehicle and assumed that he rode the bus.

"No, no bus," he replied when she asked. "Friend bring me to town in morning. Night, I find a way."

"Bobul, it's freezing out there. I can't let you just start out walking. Let me give you a ride home."

He gave a quick nod and shrugged into his gigantic coat, while Sam switched off the lights. Her remote key fob unlocked the van doors and Bobul started to take the passenger seat. Then he paused and picked up something. By the time Sam had edged into her own seat, she noticed that he was staring intently at it.

"What this is?" He stared hard at her.

The photograph she'd found at Montague's place. Her jewelry box.

"Why? Do you know something about it?" she asked.

He glanced uneasily at the picture and set it on the center console of the van as he sat down.

"It's okay. Just close your door and tell me which way to go." She started the engine and waited for him to respond.

He motioned for her to take a right turn out of the alley and another right at the first intersection. "Place is in canyon."

With several choices of canyon roads in the area, Sam hoped this wasn't going to turn into an hour-long project. She followed his cryptic instructions and found herself on winding Highway 64, eastbound.

"Two mile," he said, once they were past the turnoffs to the public picnic sites.

Sam adjusted the heater settings and touched the photo again. "Bobul? What do you know about this box?"

He slumped in his seat, staring out the side window.

"Please? It's important for me to know more about it."

Oncoming headlights around one of the sharp curves drew her attention and Sam concentrated on staying on her half of the narrow road.

"Have you ever seen the box in this picture, Bobul?" she asked, once the other vehicle had passed.

His glance edged toward her. She waited, letting the question hang in the air.

"One time, Bobul see this. Many years away. Box belong to young woman, witch. Witch get some ... some power...

some, how do you say, magic."

"From the box?"

"*Da*, the power come from the box."

"And you saw this witch use the box to create magic?"

His eyes grew wide and he nodded.

He'd specifically said that it was a young witch. And yet the woman who'd given it to Sam was very old, much older than Bobul. "Do you know where the witch got the box?"

But his attention had been drawn back to the road. He indicated a two-track path to a log cabin. "Is Bobul home."

The small structure looked decrepit, like something a homesteader might have thrown together to get through their first mountain winter. The logs were rough hewn with wide chinks filled with some whitish matter. One small window to the right of the front door, three wooden plank steps leading to a narrow porch, a tin roof over the whole thing. It looked cold and dark.

"Have you owned this place a long time?" Sam asked.

"No own." He moved his hand toward the door handle as Sam brought the van to a stop.

"Wait, Bobul. I really need to know where this box came from. Can you tell me more about the witch? Did you know her here, in Taos?"

He squirmed in his seat for a minute, then sighed. "Come inside. Is long story."

Sam glanced at the dark cabin. Was this a good idea?

But Bobul was already halfway up the steps to the porch and would soon disappear inside. And it was doubtful that she would get him to talk about this subject during their workday at the bakery—assuming he came back now that she'd questioned him about such an uncomfortable subject.

She grabbed up her pack and the photograph and followed him.

By the time she stepped into the cabin, he'd lit a kerosene lamp, revealing the one-room arrangement, with a rock fireplace against one wall, an overstuffed chair in front of it and a bed across the room. A wood-burning cookstove filled another corner—together with a shelf containing a few dishes and canned goods, and a work table with a plastic wash basin, this comprised the kitchen.

Bobul moved to the fireplace and struck a match to kindling and logs that were already in place. Within minutes, their glow began to spread and the small room turned from dark and cold to warm and friendly. She saw homey touches like a homemade quilt on the bed and a few colorful dishes on the shelves. As rustic rentals went, it was cozy.

He lit a second kerosene lamp and indicated that Sam should sit in the upholstered chair. Then he pulled a straight wooden chair up to the fire and sat down.

"The witch," he said. "Where to start story . . ."

"Did you see her here, in Taos? With the box?"

He shook his head. "I was small boy, in Romania—home country. They call the witch Lorena. Lorena young and beautiful with light hair, but her children they have died and Lorena have many bad powers—how you say . . . evil. She have wood box where she keep evil spells. She make spells to kill farm animals and make crops die. If a person try to stop her, she kill them."

"Did you see her perform one of these acts?" Sam felt her skepticism rise.

"My mother see her. Many times. She tell me. She tell me about wooden box where Lorena keep her spells. In my country, box known as Facinor. Mother make me sleep with charm under pillow, keep me safe from Lorena."

"But Lorena never really tried to hurt you, did she?"

"Village men finally go after her. One night, a full moon and very cold, much snow on mountains . . . village men kill her. I see her body when they bring her to village square. I see the wooden box, Facinor, she hold in her cold fingers."

Sam swallowed hard. A lot of women were killed after being accused of witchcraft. But in this century?

"What happened then?"

"They burn her body. Mother not let me watch. I hide in bed and listen to others cheer that witch is dead."

"And the box?" Sam asked. "If they burned it up, why does it scare you now?"

Bobul's eyes grew wide again. "Facinor survive. I see it again, in Taos. In hands of new Lorena."

"New Lorena?"

His eyes narrowed. "Legend is true. When old Lorena die, she come back as new Lorena. She come back in a new place, so her killers do not find her. Bobul see this. Bobul see her in Taos. This time she is old and wrinkle and very tiny. But she still have the box."

Bertha Martinez. Bobul believed that Bertha had come back, somehow, as the new version of a woman killed in Romania at least thirty years ago. Sam tried to wrap her mind around the story. Of course, it was impossible.

"And now this Lorena also die. Bobul know this."

He could have seen Bertha's obituary. There must be logical explanations for all of this. An old clock near the bed chimed midnight, startling her. How had the hours crept away?

"Is dangerous time in year, Miss Sam," Bobul said. "In

the long nights, many spirits roam, many rituals observed. The new Lorena will appear. She will look for Facinor, to possess the box is most important. Is a . . . how do you say, a sure thing. Burn picture of box and it go away."

Whatever part of Sam might have considered telling Bobul that she knew about the wooden box, that she in fact owned it, that idea flew out the window. In his simple way of thinking, Sam herself could be the next new Lorena. Whether it was simply the effect of the early darkness, the remote cabin, the man's childhood fears . . . there was no way she wanted to attract his superstitions into her realm.

The fire glowed, low red embers that were nearly gone.

Bobul stood and poked at them, tossing on another log and watching the flames spark up again. When he turned back to her his face seemed free of all worry.

"Now Bobul sleep. Tomorrow much chocolate to make."

Sam shook off the uneasy remnants of the story and stood. Her coat was draped over the back of the cushy chair and she snuggled deeply into it, wanting to carry the cabin's warmth with her, out into the cold night.

Chapter 17

An icy fog had settled in the depths of the canyon during the evening and Sam found herself creeping along in the van, more than a little spooked. At last she turned into her own Elmwood Lane and parked, scurrying into the house and double checking the locks. Kelly's door was closed and she'd left one lamp on in the living room for Sam. The normalcy of it should have reassured Sam. She washed her face and put on her nightshirt, repeating to herself, *it's only a silly story.* There was no way that burning a photograph would make a real object go away.

But in her bedroom she found herself pulling open the lower drawer of her dresser, checking to be sure the box was still there, benign and empty of everything except Sam's own jewelry. She laid a scarf over it and closed the drawer.

Falling into bed, she chided herself for staying out so

late and for listening to the chocolatier's wild tales. She'd forfeited four hours of valuable sleep, and having to appear at the bakery at five o'clock held no appeal right now. She closed her eyes. It had been a *very* long day.

But her sleep was sporadic and filled with odd images. In one dream, the young blond Lorena appeared, wanting to hand Sam the wooden box and asking her to take over Lorena's job as village witch. When Sam refused the box, she turned around to find Bertha Martinez on her deathbed, making the same request. She woke with a start and sat up in bed. That last scene was a little too real, since it had actually happened back in September.

Sam turned on the lamp and fiddled with her clock radio. Finding a station with soft music she turned the volume low and tried to settle back and let it lull her to sleep. It worked for about an hour, until the station format changed and jangled her nerves with a program devoted to salsa music. She slapped the radio, hard, and rolled over with the pillow over her head. She woke in that position to the persistent beep of her alarm, at four-thirty.

* * *

In the cold light of day, Bobul's story of the witch Lorena faded. Sam told herself that she'd spent many a dark night by a campfire, swapping stories designed to scare the bejesus out of kids. She didn't believe in witches, no matter what country they supposedly came from. And for the moment she had her hands full depicting the Taos Plaza in intricate detail in cake.

Becky came in late and grumpy but at least she was there.

While Becky worked to get the breakfast assortment baked and on display, Sam iced the buildings on the plaza cake with buttercream tinted the perfect shade of adobe brown. She piped details—windows and doors and even cracks in the sidewalks.

Kelly and Becky began forming little cars out of moldable chocolate and Bobul added his own expertise in shaping people for the walkways, Christmas wreaths on lamp poles, and tiny luminarias—those traditional decorations that in real life were made from paper sacks with sand and a candle in each one. The chocolatier had given Sam a cautious look when he arrived, but when she didn't ask any more questions about the witch, he lapsed back into his usual quiet mode of concentration on his work.

By noon, the plaza cake was looking good and Becky's moodiness had passed. Sam kept thinking of small details to add, but realized that she couldn't really afford to keep four people working on it when there were other projects nearly as urgent. She sent Bobul back to his chocolate creations and asked Kelly to check the status of the sales counter.

When she reported back that they had no decorated cakes, no cheesecake, and only four dozen cookies, Sam's orders began to fly.

"Becky, get cheesecakes into the oven. At minimum, we better have the amaretto, the pumpkin and a plain one. If there's time, a praline and a blueberry would be good too. And a few of the new fruitcakes. They went well. While those bake—do cookies. You know how we go through those in the afternoons. Start with the simple pressed butter varieties. Kelly can help decorate. I'll pull some of those cake layers from the fridge and get holiday designs on them.

Let's work like mad-women until two, then we better get the plaza cake delivered. I'll need at least one of you to go with me."

By the time she needed to load the large cake into the van, Sam had turned out a dozen smaller, decorated ones. She carried square and rectangular cakes, done up with fondant bows in reds and greens, red velvet cakes with snowy frosting and piped green wreaths, and winter wonderland white cakes with sugar cone pine trees and glitter dustings of snow. With this being the last week of school, scores of parties and dozens of teacher gifts were needed. Of course, that reminded her that she better also fill the cases with cupcakes.

She told Becky to get a few dozen into the oven, while Sam commandeered Kelly to help with the delivery of the plaza cake.

When they returned, a half-hour later, there was an air of exhaustion in the kitchen. Except from Bobul. The man seemed to work like a machine—an exceptionally talented machine. He'd turned out three dozen more of those tiny, exquisite pinecones.

"Let's take a little breather," Sam said to the group.

Becky and Kelly helped themselves to an unfrosted chocolate cupcake each from the cooling racks and walked to the front to see if there was any coffee left. While they filled mugs and invited Jen to join them at one of the bistro tables, Sam pulled out her order sheets for the week.

Somehow they'd gotten out of sequence and she realized that there was a bachelorette party tonight, the Southwell wedding in three days with its twelve-hundred truffles, and a gallery opening on Thursday. All that in addition to the normal load of birthdays and dinner parties that crowded the December calendar. She rubbed at the pain that was beginning to form at her temples.

"Mom, you look like you need a break," Kelly said, wiping chocolate crumbs from her lap.

"Not happening this month, I'm afraid," Sam said. She let out a pent-up breath. "Thank goodness you were available. I don't know how we'd handle it with just three of us."

Becky looked a little uncomfortable. Once her kids were out of school for the holiday break, technically she wasn't supposed to be on duty. The realization must have showed on Sam's face.

"I'll see what I can do about putting in more hours," Becky said, "but I don't know . . ."

Sam turned away, disappointed.

Bobul appeared from the kitchen, balancing a dozen one-pound boxes of his chocolates. Good thing, Sam thought, noticing that their supply from this morning was already gone. She got a momentary wilting sensation when she realized that the next two weeks would only get busier. How many people waited until a few days before Christmas, hoping to simply pop in and pick up their pastries? This first year in business was proving to be a real test.

For the next two hours, Becky baked and Sam decorated in silence. She took an otherwise-plain half-sheet cake and added a few risqué details for the bachelorette cake, going by the requests the woman's maid of honor had suggested. It was ready five minutes before the customer came in to pick it up. But five minutes was enough.

Kelly learned how to form truffles and Bobul dipped them as quickly as they could work. Despite the fact that he'd already created a sizeable stash of them, tomorrow they would have to work double-time to fill the rest of the wedding order. By closing time, Sam had finished trays of cupcake Santas, snowmen, and Christmas trees. Some went into the display cases out front, while others sat in cold storage in the walk-in refrigerator.

"I feel like a marathon runner," Jen said, breathing hard as she brought back an empty tray.

"Well, you've been dashing back and forth to keep everything stocked, all afternoon," Sam said with a smile. "Thanks."

She faced the others. "Thanks, everyone. I couldn't do it without you." She received tired smiles in return. "Let's knock off and get some rest so we can hit it again tomorrow."

No one argued. Even Bobul seemed ready to quit for the day. His work area was neat and he'd put the little packets of spices back into his tote bag.

"Mom? You're not staying late, are you?" Kelly asked. "I heard you come in last night and I know you got up early this morning. You can't wear yourself so thin that you get sick."

Sam chuckled and looked down at herself. "I'm not in much danger of wearing myself thin."

Kelly huffed and rolled her eyes. "You know what I mean."

"In answer to your question, I'm walking out the door the same time you do. Want to pick up some fast food on the way home?"

"I'll do it. You go home. Shall it be pizza, burgers or chicken?"

"Pizza."

Kelly speed dialed a number on her cell phone and rapped out quick instructions, "See ya in twenty."

Sam watched the three younger women head out toward their cars. Bobul had disappeared into the early evening gloom, as he always did. That neighbor must be pretty accommodating, giving him a ride out to the canyon every day. She locked the front door, smiled as she passed the neat cases of goodies, then walked out to her van. Her shoulders ached and her lower back felt as if she'd been kicked by a horse. But she couldn't admit that she was feeling her age—and she darn sure wasn't going to allow the thought that the bakery was proving to be a lot of work. It was still work that she loved.

She drove straight home, wondering if she might have time for a hot bath before Kelly got there with the pizza. Decided that a few ibuprofen and a glass of wine would work more quickly, so she did that instead. By the time Kelly walked in, Sam had tossed together a few salad ingredients and they sat down to their simple feast.

"Better!" Kelly declared after polishing off two slices and a plate of salad. "I feel like I might actually make it to morning."

They put away the leftovers and Kelly announced that she was going to watch one—and only one—episode of her favorite reality show, then she was going to bed.

Sam had brought home the order sheets for all their custom work for the coming week, so she sat at the kitchen table calculating to see whether she would need additional supplies of butter, sugar and flour, and what special items would be required for the two upcoming wedding cakes. The first one required fresh flowers for the top and the bride's florist was supposed to bring those over the day of the wedding, still a few days away.

The more urgent was Mira Southwell's cake, the timid bride with the ferocious mom. At least the ingredients were all standard items. Kelly trudged by, giving a little wave and a yawn on the way to her bedroom, and Sam realized that her own energy was lagging as well.

She stared, unseeing, at the piles of paperwork around her. How was she going to get all this done?

Well, there was one sure way.

She discarded the idea of using it even though Bobul's stories were ludicrous. Facinor, indeed. Lorena—ridiculous!

But the pile of work just seemed overwhelming. She stood up and stretched. Her limbs still ached. She should go to bed. She switched out the kitchen lights and headed for her bedroom with the idea that a hot bath and her cozy nightie would be just what she needed. The bath did relax her, but her mind wouldn't slow down and she couldn't let go of the idea that if she could only have the energy she used to . . .

Without thinking, she opened the bottom drawer of her dresser. The scarf over the wooden box had slipped aside and one of the red stones on the box winked at her in the lamplight.

"You don't really have a name," Sam said. "and you have never been to Romania, have you?" She picked it up.

When Bertha Martinez had handed Sam the box, the old woman told her that the box held power. That Sam could accomplish good things with it. And so far that prediction had come true. Sam held the box to her chest, feeling the warmth travel from the wood into her body. Her arms began to tingle. She dropped it back into the drawer. What was she thinking?

This box . . . this thing that both attracted and repulsed her . . .

She stared at the wood, which was glowing golden now. The red, green and blue stones were brilliant. And she felt like a twenty-year-old who'd just awakened from a great night's sleep. She shook her arms. The feeling didn't go away.

Well, there would be no sleep now.

She edged the drawer closed with her toe, then pulled on fresh clothing and tiptoed through the house. Gathering the papers from the kitchen table, she stuffed them into her pack, put on her coat and quietly left the house.

Chapter 18

Bobul was the first to arrive at the bakery in the morning. His silent gaze traveled the room.

"Have been busy, Miss Sam," he said. "Almost like magic."

Sam opened her mouth to protest, but there wasn't much she could say without giving away her possession of the box he called Facinor. And there was no way she could do that.

"I, um, just woke up early."

He shrugged his beefy shoulders and slipped out of his big brown coat. When Sam looked again, he was shaving chocolate from a rough block into a double boiler.

None of his concern anyway, she thought, grabbing large packages of cold butter from the fridge and slapping them onto the work table. So what if she'd worked all night. It was her shop; she was boss of the whole place. And if she was willing to do whatever it took to make the business successful, well, so much the better.

She looked up, taking in the two elaborately finished wedding cakes. One was five tiers of lemon-poppyseed cake, covered in buttercream, with flowers cascading from one level to the other, lilies and primroses and scatterings of tiny violets. She'd created rippled bunting along the edges of the larger tiers, string work around the smaller ones. A cake like that would have normally taken two full days to complete. It would go into the cooler until the florist brought the fresh flowers.

The Southwell cake sat beside it—four tiers draped in ivory quilt-textured fondant, with burgundy flowers and tiny edible gold beads catching the light.

And then there was the sheet cake for Thursday's gallery opening. She'd created easels and canvases from butter-cookie dough, assembled them and then, on her special printer, reproduced three miniatures of the featured artist's better-known works. The cake itself had been frosted and trimmed in the gallery's colors, with their Woodwind Gallery logo reproduced on shields of fondant on each of the four sides. It was those little surprise elements that kept customers coming back. She carried it to the refrigerator, daring anyone to question her work.

She glanced again at Bobul, wondering if he could divine her thoughts, but he seemed busily content with his chocolate. She wouldn't have been behind in her bakery orders anyway, Sam reasoned, if she'd not taken so much time worrying over William Montague. Now *that*, that was really someone else's job.

Becky came in at six. Her eyes went wide and she exclaimed at the sight of the wedding cakes, but Sam didn't go into a detailed explanation. She asked for a hand in getting them to the fridge, then sent Becky to begin the standard breakfast pastries. By the time Kelly and Jen arrived just before seven the shop was ready for the daily crowd, Sam had already placed her order online for more supplies, and she was well into the assembly of a dozen cookie trays that a local cosmetics saleslady wanted as gifts for her team members. As long as she was at it, she started an extra tray, which she would give Zoë as a thank-you for sharing her grandmother's recipes.

"Mom?" Sam caught Kelly staring at her. "You okay?"

"Yeah . . . why?" Sam looked in the mirror over the sink and saw that her face had the reddish cast of someone who'd been running a marathon and her hair stuck out at all angles.

"Did you actually sleep last night? I didn't hear you get up this morning."

Sam fudged. "Well, I just had all this stuff . . . you were probably sound asleep when I left."

"Hmm. Okay." Kelly gave her a hug. "Just don't overdo it. You've been at this for hours."

Sam noticed that the clock above the sink showed 7:49. Wow. Nearly twelve hours since she'd handled the wooden box. That was about the limit of its energy, from what she'd discovered in the past. No wonder she was looking a little peaked.

Her cell phone buzzed down in her pocket and she set aside the roll of red cellophane she'd picked up for the cookie trays. Delbert Crow.

"What's the status of the property in Talpa?" he asked. No niceties with this guy.

"It's winterized and secured. What's the status supposed to be?"

"I had an odd call late last night," he said. "A woman who claimed to be Mr. Montague's niece. She chewed me a new one because our sign is in the front yard."

"A niece? I don't know anything about that. The sign is there. I posted it like we always do."

"But this lady . . . let's see . . . her name was Tiffany Wright. She's on her way to Taos. When she gets there, can you talk to her? Find out if she plans to get the payments up to date." He rattled off a phone number which she scribbled in frosting on the surface of the table.

Why didn't you *talk to her?* Sam thought. But Crow was in no mood, after being awakened in the night. He'd already hung up.

"Like I need one more thing to do today," Sam muttered, shoving the phone back into her pocket. "Kelly, could you take over these cookie trays? Red cellophane, green satin bow. The Hanukkah ones get blue wrap, silver ribbon—"

"Sure, Mom."

"I'll take the first one with me. I'm going out anyway and I want to give it to Zoë. The others are for . . . let's see . . . the order form is here somewhere." Already Sam felt her energy slipping away as she fumbled through the pages.

"It's okay. See Zoë, get some rest. We can handle things here," Kelly said. "I'll spend the rest of the day helping Bobul finish the wedding truffles." She indicated the special boxes Sam had bought for them. Cases of completed wedding favors were stacked against one wall.

Sam copied the phone number for Tiffany Wright and wiped up the smudged frosting. It was an unfamiliar area code. So, how had Ms. Wright learned of the sign on the Montague property?

One way to find out. She dialed the number.

It took a little explaining for Tiffany Wright to understand who Sam was and why she was calling.

"I got a call from some sheriff's deputy in Taos and it kind of freaked me out." The woman sounded young and flustered. "I'm at the airport now. I should be in Albuquerque this afternoon and I'll drive up. I just can't believe Uncle William's house is in some kind of trouble."

Again, Sam wondered why Delbert Crow hadn't simply handled this himself. He was the one with the procedures manual, all the rules about who to contact and how to get a delinquent homeowner to pay up. Sam was only supposed to be the keeper of keys and mower of lawns. She gritted her teeth.

Meanwhile, the woman requested that they meet at her hotel, the Cottonwood Inn, tomorrow morning. Fine. But Sam really hoped she could hand this off to either Delbert Crow or Beau well before that.

She took a deep breath and stared at herself again in the mirror. Bags under her eyes, a feverish sheen to her skin. Kelly was right—she was exhausted. She picked up a blue-wrapped tray of cookies for Zoë and headed out the back door.

Driving home, Sam stayed on auto-pilot. This was stupid, and dangerous. What was the point of staying up all night, working at a frantic pitch, only to be completely zonked before noon the next day? Granted, she'd accomplished two days' work by herself, but at what price? She walked into the quiet house, lifted the phone off the hook and switched off her cell, then fell into bed.

When she awoke the angle of the sun told her it was mid-afternoon. With a luxurious stretch she wondered what it would be like to pull the covers over her head and stay there for about a week. But she felt wide awake, not at all dreading the fact that she still had a number of things to finish today. She took a quick shower and dressed, for the first time in a week, in something other than her bake shop attire.

The tray of cookies in their classy blue and silver wrapping waited on the kitchen counter. Sam smiled, reminding herself that the holiday season was one of joy, of fun surprises like taking a sumptuous array of treats to a friend. Just because it was a lot of work didn't mean that she couldn't enjoy herself as well.

Zoë and Darryl's bed and breakfast was decked out in full regalia. They didn't especially celebrate the religious significance of the season but it didn't mean that they weren't really into the ambiance. Darryl had hung evergreen swags around the entire porch railing. Bright red bows added punch, and Sam saw that tiny white lights in all the shrubs would sparkle after dark. She noticed a car in the guest parking area out front, so she pulled around back and entered through the kitchen.

"Hey there!" Zoë greeted. "Merry Christmas or Happy Hanukkah or whatever you want it to be. I love your sweater!"

Sam had grabbed one of her whimsical tops, a white sweater with a reindeer knitted into it, the nose done in red spangles. She handed the cookie tray to Zoë. "Your recipes. I hope they turned out right."

"They look beautiful! Here, I'd like you to meet one of our guests. Magda Hernandez, meet Samantha Sweet." The rather large woman had a tangle of dark hair, gathered back from her face and held at the crown with a silver clip. She wore a silky broomstick skirt in shades of turquoise and purple and a long-sleeved tunic that picked up the purple tones. Sam admired the strands of her turquoise heishi necklace as she stepped forward to shake Magda's hand.

"Just Sam," she said.

"Magda is here in Taos for a break from her studies. She's recently completed a Master's Degree in New Mexico tradition, with a specialty in folklore," Zoë said. "And since you're here, Sam, do you mind if we break into the cookies? I've got hot cider on the stove."

The offer was too good to pass up and Sam found plates and napkins while Zoë happily untied the bow from Sam's gift. Zoë placed the tray of cookies in the middle of her round kitchen table and brought mugs of cider while the others sat down.

Magda bit into one of the dreidl-shaped butter cookies. "Oh, this is good."

"I can second that," Zoë said. "Just like grandma's." She and Sam both chuckled.

"Magda, I heard a strange bit of folklore a couple of days ago," Sam said. "Not to make you talk shop when you're on vacation, but I wonder—"

"I don't mind a bit," Magda said. "I love my subject, or I wouldn't have spent all these years working on it. What was the story?"

Sam wasn't quite sure where to start so she began with Bobul's story of the witch Lorena he claimed to have seen as a child.

"This man swears he saw her die in Romania, and that she was a young woman at the time. Then, he says he saw the witch Lorena again in New Mexico. She was very, very old, even though not that many years had passed."

"Did he refer to her as a witch, a *bruja*, or a *curandera*?" Magda asked.

"In the childhood part of his story, he definitely used the word witch. I don't remember his using either of the Spanish words. Is there a difference?"

"In Spain, and later in the Southwestern United States, the common term is *bruja*."

Sam nodded. "I've heard that associated with, uh, someone."

"But one of the misconceptions to some people is that the name *bruja* conveys magic used for evil. The *curandera* might also use some techniques considered to be magical, but hers are always done for healing or for good."

Sam helped herself to a second macaroon. "Makes sense. Kind of."

Both Magda and Zoë were watching her closely. "Well, it's just that this person, a local woman who died awhile back—everyone called her a *bruja*. But from what I can tell, her powers were used for healing."

Sam met Zoë's gaze. Her friend had experienced the healing power of Sam's encounters with the wooden box, but Sam had never explained how it worked. Zoë sipped at her cider and didn't say anything.

"Well, it's certainly possible that rumors got started

and those who spread them really didn't know what the old woman did. There have been cases of women being tormented, even killed, for practicing what is basically just a form of natural healing. In my research I came across several cases of the so-called witch's property being stolen. She might have a book of cures, some special herbs, or even an object—maybe a container that she kept the herbs in— and people who didn't really understand how her abilities worked would go to great lengths to get their hands on these items."

An item like a box, Sam thought. She swallowed too fast and got a crumb stuck in her throat. As she sputtered and took some cider to dislodge it, Magda went on.

"Sam, you mentioned that this man called the witch in the old country Lorena. Are you familiar with the New Mexico legend of La Llorona?" Magda picked up a pencil and wrote the name on her napkin.

The double L was, of course, pronounced as a Y— Yoh-rohna, but even though the pronunciation was very different, Sam was struck by the similarities in the names.

"So . . . they're related?"

Magda sighed. "It's very possible. Folk legends tend to cross cultures and continents with a lot of their elements intact. There are several versions of the New Mexico legend, but most involve a widowed woman whose children drowned—whether by her hand or her husband's—and she wanders the lakes and rivers of the area, looking for them. Her cry is supposedly one of the most pitiful and awful things a person can hear. La Llorona is more of a ghost than a witch, but you can see how the notions of spooky things become somewhat muddled over the years."

Sam nodded. "You know, there's one other thing. This man who told me of the Lorena legend in Romania said that the witch had a wooden box that contained her spells—you mentioned something like that. He gave this particular box a name. Facinor. Have you heard of that?"

The other woman's eyebrows crinkled in concentration. "Not that particular name. However, it's a strange one. The word facinorous is a rather obsolete adjective used to describe something atrociously wicked. Like the extreme of evil." She raised one shoulder in a little shrug. "It could be that the villagers back there used such archaic terms. Maybe they heard it from an English speaker who traveled through . . . someone picked up on it, started using it in relation to the woman they burned as a witch? Hard to say exactly."

Or maybe they had a real reason to think of the box and its owner as evil. Sam put the macaroon down. She suddenly had no appetite.

Chapter 19

I don't believe it's true. I really *don't believe it's true. It isn't true.* The words ran through Sam's head all the way home from Zoë's house.

Fact: she'd owned the box for nearly three months now. Fact: nothing bad had happened to her. Fact: each time she'd handled the box she'd been suddenly able to do things that could best be described as unusual. Okay, weird. Fact: most of those things were actually good things—a more youthful appearance, extra energy, more strength, a healing touch with others. She'd met Beau. She'd come into the money to open her pastry shop. Her relationship with her daughter had improved vastly.

Okay, there were some things that might be classified as weird-but-good—seeing fingerprints that were invisible to other people, likewise with auras and reading other people's emotions.

But evil? No. She'd helped Beau solve two murders because of those special abilities.

Magda Hernandez's words came back: *People would often go to great lengths to get their hands on these items.*

Obviously, William Montague had an interest in the box. When a collector of bizarre objects has a photo of something you own, and then that person disappears . . .

A cold chill enveloped her.

She parked in her driveway, jumped out of the van and dashed inside. Without even thinking about it she turned on a light in every room and double-checked the locks on all the doors. Rushing into her bedroom she opened the bottom drawer of her dresser. The box sat exactly where she'd left it, the wood now faded back to its customary dull yellowish-brown. The colored stones were so dim it was hard to distinguish them.

Okay, this is getting ridiculous, she told herself. She slammed the drawer. *I'll be careful. I can keep the box hidden away and be cautious about letting anyone know about it.* So far, only Kelly and Beau had even seen the box. Only Beau knew any details.

In the kitchen her message light blinked. Beau's voice came on when she pressed the button. "Hey there, guess your cell phone is turned off. Call me." It reassured her to hear the normalcy of him.

She rummaged in her pack for her cell phone. He was right. She'd somehow left it turned off. He'd left an identical message on the voice mail.

"Hey you," she said when he answered. "Busy?"

"One sec." She heard some muffled noises and then he came back on. "Lucky speeder. I let him go with a warning.

I'd rather talk to you."

"Any news on the Montague case?" she asked.

She heard a car door close and the background noise dropped immediately. "Not a whole lot. Several fingerprints but other than yours and Montague's, there were no matches in the database. The vehicles in the garage are registered to him. No warrants on him or his cars. Getting into his bank accounts would take a court order and I can already tell you that no judge is going to give us one. There's just not enough evidence of any crime."

"I got an interesting call. I'm not sure if you want me to follow it up alone, though." She told him about Delbert Crow's passing along the midnight call from Tiffany Wright. "When I called her back this morning, she was in an airport, on her way to Albuquerque, then planning to drive up here. I forgot to ask where she lives, but she and I are supposed to meet at the Cottonwood Inn in the morning."

"I don't recognize the name, right off hand. She's a niece, huh?"

"Yeah. Said your deputy called her and she got scared that something has happened to Uncle William." She stared into the refrigerator, half thinking about dinner. "So, do you want to be in on the meeting with her tomorrow? Or would you rather that I didn't even talk to her?"

"I can't make it but you go ahead, if you're willing. See what you can find out. Maybe she knows some way to get in touch with him. Obviously, his friends here in town don't have much of a clue."

"I'll let you know what she has to say. Maybe we could meet for lunch tomorrow?"

With the normal disclaimers about last minute disasters, Sam pinned him down to time and place. Belatedly and with a stab of guilt, Sam remembered to ask about Iris and learned that Beau's mother was making slight improvements each day. Basically, he was dashing from work to hospital to home all the time; she almost suggested canceling lunch plans. Both of them had lots on their plates. But when he turned the conversation toward the romantic and she heard the hunger in his voice, she knew they needed to find any spare minutes that they could.

When Kelly walked in the door, a little after six, Sam had put together a hearty green chile stew, cornbread, and salad.

"Wow, Mom, this smells so good!" She handed over a zippered bank bag that felt pleasantly fat. "Great day at the store," she said, washing her hands at the sink and turning to help Sam carry bowls to the table.

They ate and cleared the kitchen, watched some TV, and Sam wrote out a bank deposit slip. By the time she got ready for bed, Sam had forgotten about the *bruja* stories and the box, and she let herself slip into a deep sleep.

* * *

"Ms Sweet, glad to meet you." The young woman who greeted Sam at the door to Room 147 held out her hand. She was definitely a city transplant, wearing a fitted black dress, a bright yellow wool jacket, and yellow pumps to match. With her chic haircut and accessories that screamed Neiman-Marcus, Sam guessed stock broker, banker or real estate agent.

"Well, I was glad to finally have contact from a relative of Mr. Montague's. You said you're his niece?"

"Yes. Could I offer you some coffee before we go out to the house?" Tiffany gestured with an elegantly manicured hand toward the tiny in-room coffee service.

Considering that she'd downed three cups since arriving at the bakery at five this morning, Sam declined. Besides, the shop's signature blend far outshone anything a motel could offer.

"You're probably smart to pass," Tiffany said, as if she'd read Sam's mind. "It's not all that great."

They took seats in a pair of uncomfortably straight chairs, on either side of a small round table.

"So, how is it that you and Mr. Montague are related?"

"I'm his—oh, I see what you mean. His sister was my mother. We stayed in Chicago when he moved out west. Mom always thought it strange that he chose such a small town, after being raised with all the conveniences of a big city."

"Do they stay in touch?"

"Oh, my mother passed away five years ago. Breast cancer. It was a tough time, and since then I just haven't been as good about contacting him."

"When was the last time you heard from him?"

"Oh, gosh . . ." Her eyes rolled upward, staring at a spot on the ceiling. "I can't exactly remember. Months, at least. Maybe sometime last spring. He always called on my birthday. So, that would have been April."

"Are there other relatives who might have heard from him more recently than that? Someone he might ask to handle his finances if he were unavailable?"

"No, I don't think so. I can take over those things once I get the key to the house and have access to his records. It did rather surprise me when a sheriff's deputy from Taos called to say that the house was about to go into foreclosure. I mean, letting his payments fall behind would not be at all like Uncle William."

"I'm afraid I'm not at liberty to hand over the keys and let you remove anything from the house," Sam said. "It's a matter of first finding out if Mr. Montague is dead or alive."

Tiffany blanched a little at that.

"I'm sorry. I shouldn't have been so blunt." Sam reached her hand across the table. "I didn't mean—"

"It—it's all right. I just assumed that a sheriff's phone call to next of kin meant that he'd died. I had no idea—"

Sam watched the young woman's face. Odd that she seemed more shocked by the idea that her uncle might still be alive, than the possibility of his death.

Tiffany seemed to realize that Sam was watching her rather intently. She excused herself and got a tissue from the dispenser in the bathroom vanity and came back rubbing at her nose. She stood near the room's one bed, sniffing at the tissue with her back turned to Sam.

"Well, I suppose I should still go out there—to the house, I mean. To check on his things, make sure everything is all right."

"Actually, that's what my job is," Sam told her. "I've been out there several times since the first of the month. The house is safely winterized and secure."

Tiffany turned toward Sam, her face completely dry.

"Ms Wright, I'm only authorized to talk to you about a payment plan, if you're interested in stepping in on your uncle's behalf to get the mortgage up to date. In arrears, the next step is for the department to sell or auction the house and contents, I believe. Of course, my supervisor in the USDA office would actually handle the paperwork."

"He had some things that belong to me. I need to retrieve them." Her voice had taken on a desperate edge.

"Fine," Sam said, pulling her cell phone from her pocket. "I'll arrange for the sheriff to meet us there."

Tiffany's face went two shades paler. "Um, you know, I better check my itinerary. Make sure we can find a mutually agreeable time."

Sam held the phone up. "We can ask him now."

The younger woman stepped over to the nightstand and picked up her own cell phone. "Sorry. It just vibrated." She opened it and held it up to her ear, nodding.

Sam kept her seat until Tiffany turned to her. "I'm really sorry. This is business. It's going to take awhile. I'll get back to you."

With a condescending smile, she walked Sam to the door and held it open. It clicked firmly shut behind Sam's back.

"*This* is business," Sam sing-songed. "Hah—this is b.s. That phone didn't ring."

She'd parked the bakery van right outside the room so there was no unobtrusive way to stake out Ms Wright. She cranked the ignition and backed out. At the end of the row of rooms, she pulled around the corner of the building, turned the van to face the direction she'd come from, and dialed Beau's number.

"Montague's *niece* is quite a pushy little thing," she said before he'd barely said hello.

"You think it's one of those middle aged man/younger woman relationships? That kind of niece?"

Sam thought about that. "I doubt it. She didn't seem at all genuinely concerned for him. She'd arrived here assuming he was dead and wanting me to just hand over the keys to his house."

"Well, it *is* a pretty nice house," he said, with a hint of humor.

"I can just see Ms Wright waltzing in there and cleaning the place out."

"Well, it's a little more difficult than that, Sam. If Montague is dead, there must be a will, probate, the whole court system getting into it. She would have to be named as his heir."

"*If* it's done by the book," she reminded him. "You've never heard of someone just clearing out a house, whether they had the right to or not?"

"Let me do a little more checking before we jump to conclusions," he said. "I'll call you—"

"Wait, Beau!" Sam caught movement down the row of rooms. A bright yellow jacket moved toward a red sedan. "She's getting into a car. What shall I do? I can't very well follow her in the bakery van. She's already seen it."

There was a moment of silence, and Sam watched Tiffany back out of her parking spot. She put the van in gear, just to be ready.

"Stick with her, maybe a block or so back, until one of my guys can pick up the tail. She may be heading for Montague's house."

"My thought exactly. I could get there ahead of her. There's a back way that bypasses all the traffic."

"Sam, let us handle this. Just stay on the phone, keep her in sight and let me know where she is."

"For starters, she's taking a left, southbound onto Paseo.

I'll get myself out there."

She edged the van around the motel, paused near the portico where incoming guests came, then headed toward the driveway. She spotted two red sedans about two blocks away already, and she couldn't tell which was Tiffany's. She whipped out into traffic, narrowly missing a garbage truck.

"Beau, I see her up ahead, but there are two similar cars. I'm not sure if she's the first one or the second." No response. "Beau?"

Something clicked in her ear and he was back. "Sorry, I got on the radio. If she passes the intersection at Cervantes, Joe will pick her up. He's just pulling out of the high school and can be there in under a minute."

"Tell him she's wearing a bright yellow jacket. That'll help him know which of the red cars is hers." Sam accelerated and got within four car lengths of her target when the traffic slowed down. Craning her neck, she made out Tiffany's distinctively shaped hairstyle. The logo on the car was Nissan. She passed that information along to Beau.

Two more blocks and she saw the deputy's car pull out. When the road widened he stayed with the one in the right hand lane. No lights, no siren, just a steady tail, and it didn't take long for Tiffany to become rattled. When she pulled off into the Walmart parking lot, Sam knew she'd given up on the idea of driving straight to Montague's house.

"She won't give up forever, though," she told Beau. "If she came all the way out here from Chicago—assuming that part of the story wasn't a total lie—she's not leaving this easily."

He huffed out a breath. "I guess I ought to post someone out at the house. But I sure don't have the extra manpower to put a guy on long-term guard duty. About all we can do is patrol past it a few times a day."

She knew he was thinking how useless that would be. Tiffany could completely ransack the place—assuming she wasn't afraid of breaking a nail—well before the understaffed sheriff's department could catch her.

Chapter 20

Sam fidgeted while she spent the remainder of the morning decorating cakes with Christmas bows, snowflakes, Stars of David. With a week to go before Christmas customers were cleaning out the displays as fast as she could fill them but Sam's mind was on the odd conversation she'd had with Montague's niece Tiffany. It bothered her that the woman had pushed so hard to get into his house. She sighed. At least she'd reported it to Beau and he seemed concerned enough to keep tabs on things.

Becky continued to bring a steady supply of cake layers from the oven, cooling them in the walk-in fridge where Sam retrieved them to decorate. On her next trip, she spotted the elaborate art cake for the Woodwind Gallery party and remembered that she had to deliver it sometime this afternoon. The day was simply getting too busy.

When Kelly walked into the kitchen to restock the cupcake supply in the displays, Sam asked for a hand. The two of them carried the large sheet with its edible easels out to the van where it would stay cool.

"Thanks, Kel," she said, closing the doors. "I'll deliver this before I meet with Beau."

While Sam added piped borders onto the last two cakes on the work table, Becky was dotting eyes and noses on a tray of Santa cookies, and Bobul as usual was in his own little world, shaping truffles and dipping them in white chocolate.

Sam caught herself thinking again of William Montague as she drove the three blocks to the gallery on the plaza. She parked next to a red curb and hoped that she could plead mistaking it for a delivery zone if she were questioned. Parking spaces on the plaza were always at a premium, more so this time of year, and there was no way to wrestle the huge cake any distance of more than a few yards.

She poked her head into the Woodwind and called out. The owner, a thin man of about thirty-five, with a perpetually bored expression, raised his head.

"I need assistance with the cake," she said. "At least one person?"

He lifted his chin and snapped his fingers toward the back of the room. A young woman appeared, brushing dust from her hands. She spotted the bakery van and guessed what the mission was, so she pulled one of those moist towelettes from a plastic canister and wiped the residual grime off. The man made no move to join them.

"Take this end, please," Sam said, tugging the length

of the cake toward the open doors. Together, they got it balanced and managed to stop traffic as they crossed back to the gallery.

"Oh, this is marvelous," the owner gushed as he handed Sam the check for the balance. "Our guests will be so impressed."

Sam smiled and tucked the check into her pocket.

"Is William Montague one of the guests?" she asked, wondering why that had popped out, the minute she said it.

"Montague? Hardly."

"I thought he was well regarded in art circles here."

"That *internet* purveyor?" The man's nose seemed to get longer as he stared down it. "The man has handled some nice pieces, I'll grant you that. But no one would actually legitimize him as a true art dealer."

Uh-huh. "You haven't seen him around town recently, have you?"

"Ms Sweet, please tell me you aren't actually going to buy from him. You know that I'd offer you the private discount that we reserve for our best clients. I mean, after you've provided this masterpiece." He gestured toward the cake. "But to answer your question, no. I've not seen Mr. Montague in weeks."

She bit her lip, trying to think of a way to ask just how many weeks, but then she spotted a meter maid out by her van.

"Thanks. Gotta run."

By the time Sam dashed into the café where she'd agreed to meet Beau, after talking the officer out of a ticket, she had a slight sheen of sweat along her hairline, despite the fact that the temperature hadn't yet hit forty.

"You look a little bitty bit flustered," Beau said, holding her chair out for her.

She fanned her face with the menu, sending her hair outward in short spikes. "You might say that. I just came from another delivery. Can't complain though. For our first holiday season in business, it's good that we're swamped with orders."

A server with blond hair ponytailed back and a generous scattering of pimples across her jawline stepped over to take their orders.

"I had a few minutes in the office," Beau said. "Flipped through Montague's address book, and I think you'll find this interesting. There's no Tiffany Wright listed."

"His *favorite* niece, the one he calls every year on her birthday?"

"In fact, no one with the last name of Wright."

"Not a strong family lineage, then?" Sam couldn't resist the slight sarcasm.

"My deputy never called her. Looks like you were right about her being a fake."

"So, how did she find out that he's missing?"

"Now that, I can't tell you. No idea. But, it sure is interesting don't you think?"

"Definitely." She told him about the gallery owner's opinion of Montague. "I find it odd, the discrepancies in the man's image. Rupert talked about him like he was the true collector's collector—a man who knew everything about art. Now this gallery guy speaks like Montague is the scum of used-art salesmen."

"Professional jealousy?"

"Could be." Sam puzzled over it while their waitress set

plates in front of them.

"I'll tell you what I am going to do," Beau said as he picked up his sandwich. "I'm running a full background check on Montague. Whatever family ties we can dig up, whatever his history is—we will find it."

Sam bit into her sandwich—turkey with Swiss cheese and green chile—and closed her eyes. While the flavors blended in her mouth she let the puzzle of William Montague fade for a few moments.

Twenty minutes later they stood at the sidewalk, discreetly holding hands within the folds of Sam's coat. It wasn't as if the whole town hadn't figured out that the sheriff was dating the baker, but some old-fashioned sense of decorum prevailed at times.

"Is there anything I can do to help?" Sam asked. "Today and tomorrow are probably my last relatively sane days at the shop, maybe until after the new year, unless Becky gets her babysitter problems resolved so she can work."

Beau started to say something, then flinched at the vibration of his phone down inside a pocket. He let go of her hand and raised an index finger while he reached for it. After about a minute of listening, interspersed with uh-huhs and rogers, he hung up.

"They're coming out of the woodwork now," he said in a low voice.

Sam felt her eyebrows rise.

"Relatives of William Montague. Now, there's a brother. My deputy reached him from a number in the address book and he wants to come up here and find out what's going on. He's flying in from San Diego and should be here this afternoon."

At least this one might actually be legit.

"Joe also ran the plates on the red car Tiffany Wright was driving. Not a rental. It's registered to a Global Imports Company in, believe it or not, Albuquerque. I'll see what background I can get on Tiffany and the company while I'm digging up info on Montague."

"The offer of help still stands," Sam said.

"Well, since you have the keys to his place, it would be helpful if I had his business files. Can you box up those that were in the drawer and bring them by so I can take a look?"

She nodded.

"On second thought, take them to your place. Without warrants and such I'll be walking on thin ice with the department."

Gladly, Sam thought, as she walked to her van. Going back to Montague's place alone gave her a weird feeling now, knowing what was behind the bookcases. Not to mention that sitting in the chilly house for hours looking through files had little appeal. Packing them up to take home was preferable.

She wove through the congested plaza streets, fidgeting at the stop-and-go on the town's two-lane main road. She'd almost passed the Cottonwood Inn when it occurred to her that she might still learn something more about Tiffany Wright.

Not surprisingly, the red sedan was nowhere to be seen near room 147. Sam whipped around to the front of the building and stopped under the portico, without a clue what her story would be when she got inside. Luckily, that part of it worked out when she recognized the desk clerk on duty as a friend of Kelly's from her school days.

"Larry Montoya, I didn't know you worked here."

He struggled to place her until she reminded him.

"I talked to one of your hotel guests this morning, a Tiffany Wright. I need to give her something and didn't see her car outside her room."

Larry clicked a few computer keys. "Sorry, Ms Sweet, she checked out right before noon."

"Rats, I was afraid of that. Can you give me her home address so I can mail this, uh, item to her?"

His eyes widened. "We aren't allowed to do that, Ms Sweet."

Sam lowered her voice to a fraction above a whisper. "I know. But I really need to get this item back to her."

"The hotel could mail it for you," he said. "We do that with things that guests leave in their rooms."

She gritted her teeth. Couldn't the bonehead see that she was bluffing? "Larry, I've known you since you were six years old, and I can still place a call to your mother."

He actually blanched. He clicked the computer mouse and a printer whirred to life behind him. "Don't ever tell anyone." Like a thief in the night he whipped the page off the printer and slid it, face down, across the desk at her.

Sam put on her brightest smile. "Thanks so much. And tell your mom hello for me." She grabbed up the paper, folded it in half and walked out. Locked inside her van she read the copy of Tiffany's hotel bill. The address was on State Street in Chicago, probably a fake. No mention of Global Imports in Albuquerque. Well, the girl had certainly covered her tracks, at least partially.

So, what to do next, she debated. Might as well go out

to Montague's place and get the files Beau had requested. She turned and looked into the van's cargo compartment. Sure enough, there was an empty shipping box she'd meant to take home with her. That would work. She took a side street and followed the back roads out to Talpa.

Fresh tire tracks made an arc in the mud in front of the large wooden gate at the Montague home. Sam parked somewhat away from them and got out to take a look. It didn't appear that anyone had actually opened the gate and driven through. With the walk-through gate it was harder to tell. She and Beau and his deputies had all entered the property over the last few days, but whether Tiffany—if that was even her real name—had come out here, she couldn't be sure.

Until she got to the front door. The lockbox she'd hung there was still in place, but the door had taken a beating. It looked like someone had hammered at the lockbox, knocking it against the carved door in an attempt to get the key out of it. Sam tugged at it, but the sturdy metal box held. That was good. She walked around the full circumference of the house, expecting to find a window bashed out, but all the entrances were intact.

She debated calling Beau to tell him about the attempted break-in but since it didn't appear that the intruder had succeeded, she figured it could wait. She picked up her cardboard box and fished out the key she always carried with her.

Inside, the house appeared just as she'd left it. Chilly. Even with the heat back on, she'd left the thermostats set just warm enough to keep the pipes from freezing. With all that granite and stainless steel, it felt like a morgue. She kept her coat on and went to the study, where she pulled open the desk drawer and lifted the file folders into the box. She caught herself glancing nervously toward the bookcases but they sat solidly in place, not even tempting her to find the switch and open the hidden room. *No sir, not me*, she thought.

Leaving the box of files beside the door, Sam made her customary rounds, checking all windows and doors, signing the sheet on the counter. Nothing seemed out of place. If Tiffany Wright had been the one who tried to break the lockbox, she'd given up pretty easily. Sam wondered what that meant as she hefted her box of papers, locked up and went to the van. Was Tiffany the real art thief or was she simply making inquiries on behalf of someone else? Someone at Global Imports, perhaps?

Chapter 21

A call to Sweet's Sweets reassured Sam that the girls had everything under control. Kelly told her that Becky was still in a little bit of a pout over the holiday work arrangements but was cranking out an amazing number of cookies and cupcakes anyway. She told Sam not to worry about getting right back—things were going fine.

Sam's lunch conversation with Beau and her discoveries about Tiffany Wright occupied her mind, so she decided to go home with the box of files and see if she could find anything that might be useful. She plopped the box onto the kitchen table and turned the heat on under the tea kettle, then took off her coat and came up with two pieces of wonderfully sticky rugelach to go with the tea.

Stacking the folders on the table, Sam wasn't exactly sure

what she was looking for. Odds were good that most of Montague's business records were on his computer, the one that they'd not found. If someone with Global Imports was behind William Montague's disappearance, they probably already had all the information they needed. They may have sent Tiffany to Taos to grab up the actual artworks, now that they knew what the collection consisted of. The girl had certainly been pushy about trying to get into the house, right from the start.

The kettle whistled and Sam took a minute to select a flavored tea and watch it darken the water in her mug. Finally, there was nothing to do but dig into the files and see what they revealed.

There were the standard business files that she suspected everyone kept: one labeled Paid Bills, one for Tax Returns, one for Sales Invoices, and something about website design. A quick glance in each, and then she laid it aside. Halfway through the stack she came to an unlabeled folder.

Interesting.

The file contained a half-inch thick stack of two-part forms, a white copy and yellow copy of each. She picked up the first one. It appeared that one or two other sheets had been torn from the back. The printed form was headed with the title: Consignment Agreement. It was a short legal document, apparently between Montague and a customer whose name was typed on a blank line and whose signature appeared, alongside William Montague's, at the bottom. Sam scanned the fine print.

It was simple enough; the customer was agreeing to place the listed pieces of artwork on consignment with Montague, who would sell the piece and earn a commission.

It all looked normal enough as far as she could tell. Even the exorbitant commission rate must have been agreeable—the customers had all signed them.

What she found interesting, though, was that as she began to read the filled-in blanks, she started to recognize some of the descriptions. The paintings and sculptures were the very ones she and Rupert had inventoried in Montague's home, the art that seemed to be his own really wasn't.

She let the pages slip back into the folder and took a sip of her tea, which was heading toward tepid.

Odd, but is it illegal? she wondered as she munched on the last rugela. Unless Montague actually kept the artworks was he really doing anything wrong? Most dealers would either keep the pieces in a storeroom or display them in a gallery. Montague was simply displaying them in his own home. There probably wasn't anything wrong with that. If his buyers paid a visit, they could view the art tastefully displayed; if they bought through his website, that was okay too. So why did the whole thing feel so weird?

Why did Tiffany Wright come this far to get her hands on the art, and then leave without trying to bluff her way through the rest of the charade? Why did some in the art community, like Rupert and Bunny Fitzhugh, seem to adore Montague, while others like the Woodwind Gallery owner reviled him? And of course Sam's thoughts went back to the hidden room with its eerie assemblage of things that could hardly be called art—was that stuff also for sale or was it Montague's own little fetish-like collection?

She poured out the cool tea and rinsed her fingers at the sink, then stacked Montague's files back in the box. She would simply have to let Beau work it out. For now, she needed to get back to the bakery and make sure things were on track.

As if by some kind of ESP, her phone rang just as she was slipping her coat on and she saw that it was Beau.

"Things go okay?" he asked. "I mean, getting the files?"

She told him about the condition of the battered front door and lock box, but assured him that nothing inside had been touched and that she now had the files safely at her home.

"Good. Maybe I can get by there tonight to take a look?"

Which led to her asking him to plan on having dinner with them, stated as she opened the freezer door in hopes of finding something easy to defrost and quick to cook. He agreed, a little distracted as someone in the office spoke to him.

"Sorry. I've got someone here. It's Will Montague's brother. You want to come by? You might think of some questions to ask him."

"You sure it's okay?"

It didn't take a lot of convincing. Sam was out the door in under a minute, parking her van on Civic Plaza Drive ten minutes later.

Whatever she thought William Montague's brother might be, she wasn't expecting what she saw. Whereas Will, in photos anyway, came across as elegantly casual in an international playboy sort of way, his brother was a ramrod-straight, crew-cut stiff military man. He wore civilian clothing—khaki slacks with a razor crease, a fresh white shirt and a pullover sweater in dark blue—but she could see career Army written all over him. He and Beau might have been colleagues, their bearings were so similar.

Beau introduced her to Robert Montague, explaining her involvement as caretaker of the house. It turned out his branch of service was Navy. She caught a strong undercurrent of concern as he greeted her.

"Rob and I were just talking about his brother," Beau said, taking his seat behind his desk. Sam and Rob Montague took the two chairs in front of it.

"I haven't seen my brother in a couple of years," Robert said. "We would talk every few months, but we weren't really close. The last time we spoke was probably around the end of the summer."

"You knew that he worked from home, dealing in art through a website?"

"Oh, yes. Will was quite the collector. Took after our mother that way. She was the art and music lover, my dad was twenty years in the Navy. I'm almost there myself, another five to go."

"I understand that Will lived in Chicago before coming to New Mexico?" Beau had a notepad on his desk but hadn't written anything on it yet.

Robert confirmed that and added that his brother would have loved to be as wealthy as his clientele, free to travel the world and live the jet-set lifestyle, but he'd never made it quite that big.

"He was involved with a woman named Bunny Fitzhugh at one time," Robert said. "I got the idea that he thought she might be his ticket. He kind of neglected to tell me that she was married until after she'd already dumped him. Of course, he didn't really put it that way. Will always had to save face, always made it sound like leaving a relationship or not going to Cannes was his idea. He never let on that the rich crowd really didn't accept him."

"That had to be hard," Sam said, thinking of the photos of Will on a ski slope with an arm around a beautiful woman, another picture on a beach with a different one.

"Does the name Wright mean anything?" Beau asked. "Any family by that name, even distant relatives?"

Rob shook his head. "No. None."

"What about a woman, probably in her late twenties, named Tiffany?"

"Not that I know of."

"Global Imports? We think they are located in Albuquerque."

Again, he shook his head. "What's this all about?"

Beau gave him the condensed version of the claims by Tiffany Wright, with Sam filling in a few details. Montague seemed genuinely puzzled by it all.

"Her story is bogus," Robert finally said. "Will and I have no sister and I've never heard of a Tiffany, in any connection. I visited Will in Chicago a few times and never met anyone of that description."

Wow, the woman who'd played the part was certainly smooth, Sam thought.

"You didn't give her his art, did you?"

"Oh, absolutely not," Beau said. "No one's getting that until and unless their claim is proven beyond a doubt."

Sam piped up. "There's something that even you don't know yet, Beau."

He sent her a guarded look. "What's that?"

"I found agreements for a lot of the art pieces in that house. They were not Will's. They were placed with him on consignment."

Beau processed the information a little more slowly

than Robert did.

"Doesn't surprise me," Rob said. "As I told you, Will didn't have a whole lot of money. He loved the lifestyle and the appearances, but he could have never afforded any really valuable art."

Sam thought back to the values Rupert had suggested for some of the pieces. Rob's statement made sense.

"So, what happens next?" Rob asked Beau.

"We can't officially do anything unless someone files a missing person report. I assume you'll be willing to do that?"

"Of course."

"We've made one quick inspection of his home, just to see whether there could have been foul play."

Rob sat forward in his chair.

"I'll let you know that there was some blood. But the results weren't conclusive." Beau reached into his desk drawer and pulled out a form. "Once he's officially reported missing, we can dig further, get search warrants, do more to find out what happened. If you can give us a DNA sample, we can check it against the blood to narrow down whether it even belongs to your brother."

While Robert Montague went through the report with Beau, Sam's mind flitted over other possibilities. She wanted to ask questions but wasn't sure how much Beau wanted to discuss in front of the so-far only known relative of a man who might very well have been murdered.

When Montague stood to leave, Sam tapped Beau on the hand. "The USDA?"

"Oh, yeah. Ask him."

"The whole reason I came to be at your brother's

home in the first place was because he'd fallen behind in his mortgage payments. The house was presumed to be abandoned and will probably go up for sale at auction." She felt strange addressing this with the clean-cut man—usually her properties were abandoned by people in much more dire straits. "It's just that, I don't know . . . if you could get the payments caught up . . . or just find out if there's money in Will's accounts to make them . . ."

"I will look into it," Rob said. "Is there a way to stall the sale? Just for a little while?"

She assured him that she would present the facts to her supervisor and do her best.

Rob Montague pulled a camel hair jacket with gold buttons from the coat rack in the corner. As he shrugged its well-cut sleeves over muscled arms he said, "Thank you. I don't know what to make of this whole thing. It's hard to believe my brother is probably dead."

Sam nodded. There wasn't a whole lot to say to that.

Chapter 22

Friday and Saturday passed in a blur, between wedding deliveries and keeping up with the daily crush at the bakery. And Sam couldn't get the conversation with Robert Montague out of her head. She wanted to believe that his concern for his brother was real, but there had been so many false leads already. At least, as Beau pointed out when they lay together in his bed after luxurious Saturday night sex, Rob had willingly filled out and signed the missing person report and he'd not tried to get his hands on the artwork. That was further than they'd gotten with the mysterious Tiffany, who'd managed to vanish from the radar.

"Have you heard anything more on your inquiries about Tiffany or Global Imports?" Sam asked.

"No, and I'm not even calling the office to find out until

Monday morning." He rolled over and began to nibble at her ear. She ran her fingertips down the length of his thigh and all other thoughts vanished for the rest of the night.

Snow had fallen during the night and they awoke to a couple of inches of white draped over the landscape. Sam sat at the breakfast table, staring out at the open fields, watching Beau's two dogs, Nellie and Ranger, as they leapt through small drifts. Beau was stirring something at the stove and he appeared at her side a minute later with plates of beautifully prepared eggs benedict.

"Wow, you *are* a good Saturday night date! Remind me to keep you around," she said.

He gave her a kiss that tasted like strawberry, then went to the kitchen and brought back a whole bowl of red, ripe ones.

Sam forced herself to take small bites and savor the eggs, Canadian bacon and sauce, although she could have easily wolfed the whole plateful in a few minutes. She would never say it to Beau but it was very nice having the house to themselves, breakfasting in their robes, not having to be conscious of appearances the way she always was with his mother around. Even though Iris was a spunky senior, who had actually encouraged the two of them to get together, certain things just didn't feel right.

As for her own parents, Sam hadn't yet worked up the courage to tell them much about Beau, certainly not that they were sleeping together. Her father would have been okay with it—he tended to accept all things as they came along, which was a good thing, since Sam's mother dished out a lot. Nina Rae Sweet wasn't mean spirited, just a little heavy-handed. Okay—sharp and preachy. And the volume of her Southern voice carried—way more than she meant it to. Howard Sweet had long ago learned to just nod and say 'yes dear' no matter what the conversation was about.

She looked over at Beau as he mopped up the last of his hollandaise sauce. She was glad that the bakery had given her the perfect excuse not to go home for Christmas this year, that she and Beau could celebrate their first one together without the drama of her family on the scene.

"I can't believe it's just a week until Christmas," Sam said, nesting her coffee mug between her hands as Beau cleared the table. The dogs had settled on the covered porch, shaking the loose snow from their coats, licking at chunks of it that had stuck to their feet. "Since it's on a Sunday this year, I'm posting notices that we'll be open only a half-day on Saturday. I hope that works. I have a feeling that people will push it, thinking they can get their pies and desserts at the last minute. But I swear, I'm out of there at one o'clock."

Beau chuckled as he joined her at the table. "Yeah, right. I can see some little old lady showing up as you're locking the door. There's no way you'd turn her down, even if you had to pop into the kitchen and bake up her special request."

"Yeah, and she'll probably be using a walker and I'll even deliver the cake and give her a ride home in the process. Just call me sucker."

He reached for her hand and squeezed it. "I love that about you, your kindness."

So maybe some of Nina Rae's preaching about manners had stuck. Sam had to admit that she had a hard time being forceful.

About the time it looked like Beau was going to really get all mushy, his phone rang. He groaned and headed toward the kitchen.

He came back after a couple minutes, tightening the sash on his robe. "Well, it doesn't seem to matter that I officially have a day off. Two deputies who live in the higher elevations where the snow's a lot deeper couldn't make it to work so I need to get into town. You're welcome to stay here and wait for me, but it may be a long day."

"No, I better just have you give me a ride home. I'll retrieve my truck and get some extra work done at the shop." She walked to the front of the house and stared down the long drive. A stone fence had created some drifts but, overall, conditions didn't look too bad.

Thirty minutes later they'd showered and dressed, and Beau insisted that Sam wait inside while he swept the snow from his official county SUV and let the heater begin to produce some warm air. It was slow going as they headed toward town. Several vehicles were off the sides of the road, apparently late-night travelers who probably should have skipped the last call at the bars. Beau switched on his strobes and pulled over at each one, checking to be sure no one was frozen inside. Luckily, they were all abandoned.

Once they passed the intersection that led to the Pueblo, the town streets showed signs of more traffic. Road crews had sanded the intersections, although there was little evidence of problems.

Sam rode along quietly as Beau took radio calls. Taos winters enchanted her. Although this snow would melt off quickly, she delighted in the view as they passed the plaza. White ridges on adobe walls, houses with their traditional blue doors that stood in bright contrast to the damp brown adobe, pine trees that could have posed for Christmas cards, evergreen wreaths with sugar-like sprinkles on them, and the tan luminarias that topped the roofline of the entire plaza. She rolled her window down a few inches and took a breath of the ice crystals that floated through the air.

Beau turned down Sam's lane and made his way carefully toward her driveway.

"Are you sure you want to go right back out?" he asked, eyeing the undisturbed expanse of white.

She looked at the snow on her truck and driveway. Staying in for the day was a lot more tempting.

"I'll think about it. Maybe later."

"I know better than to try to talk you out of it, but be careful." He leaned over to kiss her as she reached for her door handle.

Inside, Kelly was snuggled into a corner of the sofa with some weepy woman's movie on the tube. She smiled up at Sam and went right back to dabbing her eyes with the corner of her blanket.

On the kitchen table sat the box of files from Montague's place. She and Beau had gone through them carefully Friday night and he'd taken the ones he needed for his case. At some point she should take the rest back and put them in the desk, but a ride out to Talpa didn't seem very appealing. She spotted a note next to the file box.

"Kel? What's this?" It was a scrap of newspaper with Kelly's handwriting trailing around the margins.

"Some lady called. Something about a cake for her party."

Sam turned the note around, reading the string of words. Bunny Fitzhugh. Her heart stopped. Bunny's winter party cake was due this afternoon and she'd completely forgotten it. She let out an expletive and grabbed up the coat and pack that she'd just shed.

"Mom?"

"I gotta go. Call this woman back and tell her that I *will* have the cake there on time."

"What if she has a ques—"

But Sam was out the door. She grabbed up an old broom she kept on the service porch, gave two angry swipes at the snow on her truck and flung the broom to the ground. The big red pickup groaned into four-wheel-drive and the oversized wheels chewed their way down the long driveway and onto the road.

Sam's thoughts flew. What time had Bunny said she needed the cake? It was after ten already—how on earth was she going to bake, cool, decorate and deliver the thing on time? Normally it wouldn't matter if the dessert arrived after the guests were there, but she remembered Bunny saying she wanted the cake to be the centerpiece of the table. Maybe she should have taken an extra minute to call upon the powers of the wooden box, but there wasn't time to go back for it now. She was on her own.

She steered onto Kit Carson Road, pleased to see that it was slushy now. A fender-bender at the next intersection forced her to make a right turn and go two blocks out of her way but she forced herself to go cautiously. She could *not* afford to be out of commission now.

Sweet's Sweets was on night-mode, the holiday decorations and window displays adding a note of cheer to the otherwise dark shop. Sam drove to the alley in back and parked by the door, her shoes filling with snow as she leaped down from the truck. She rushed in, switching on lights and turning on the oven.

A frantic search through the pending orders revealed

that Sam's notes for Bunny's cake had gotten shuffled to the wrong stack somehow. She stomped around the work table once, cursing at the incompetence of everyone in the place, then forced herself to relax. It had been a crazy month and no one was any more to blame than herself. She was just trying to keep up with too many things at once. At least she now had the right equipment and large ovens to get all the layers done at once. Had this been last year, when she was working out of her home, she would have had to scale the design way back or admit to the customer that she couldn't fill the order. In the case of someone as well connected as Bunny Fitzhugh, it would have been a business disaster.

All these thoughts ran through her head as she dumped ingredients into the huge mixing bowl and started blending them. While the hexagon-shaped layers baked, she tinted fondant a wintry ice-blue and whipped up the basic icings she would need. Her hands were too shaky for fine detail work like piping, and every time she looked at the clock the problem got worse.

She thought about calling Kelly for extra help, but she hadn't really taught her daughter the finer points of decorating yet, and Becky, who was a wonder with the pastry bag already had attitude problems about working when she was supposed to get days off. Sam shook out the tension in her arms and sat for a minute at her desk, hands in her lap, doing a mini-meditation to calm herself down. When the oven timer went off, she felt better.

While the cakes cooled in the fridge, she rolled fondant, cut out snowflakes, and cut strips of white fondant to form into a gigantic bow for the cake's topper. Then she lined up the tools she would need to put it all together. She'd originally told Bunny that she would deliver the cake by noon, but that just wasn't happening. The open house started at four and Sam was beginning to feel like she might make that deadline. She pulled the cakes from the cooler and began to frost and decorate like she'd never done before.

At 3:42 she rolled up the driveway to Bunny's mountainside villa, thankful that the snowfall had, indeed, melted away. She was a little out of breath and certain that she had dabs of frosting on her face, but she was there and it didn't appear that the guests had arrived yet. She spotted a caterer's truck on the north side of the house and pulled her own in next to it.

Staff people were bustling about with huge trays and sprigs of evergreen for the tables, and Sam was able to talk one of the men into helping her maneuver the large cake up the inclined walkway. When they made it to the door without slipping and creating a real disaster, she breathed a sigh of relief.

Don't ever get yourself into another pinch like this, she told herself.

The caterer seemed in charge of setting out the lavish buffet—as Bunny herself was nowhere in sight—and she pointed Sam toward the table where the cake was to be.

"You're running late," the sharp-faced woman noted. "We've had to hold off the decorations because everything on this whole table is based around your piece."

Sam shot her a look. *You've never had a crisis in your business?* But she didn't say it.

Bunny's voice interrupted, high and excited, from the front hall. "Darling! So *wonderful* to see you!"

Sam craned her neck and caught a quick glimpse of a

slender figure in an emerald green jumpsuit with wide gold belt, embracing Bunny, exchanging air kisses. The woman's dark hair caught her attention. She knew that haircut.

Chapter 23

Sam started to head toward the two women, wanting to say something to Tiffany Wright, although she hadn't a clue what that would be. The caterer with the ferret-like pointed nose stopped her.

"Where are you going?" she demanded. "We don't mingle."

Sam's mouth flapped open but she was interrupted by one of the younger staff members.

"Excuse me, ma'am? Is the red truck yours?"

Sam nodded mutely.

"Another delivery is here and they need for you to move your vehicle." The girl said it apologetically, with one eye on her boss.

"Sure, no problem." Sam backed out of the dining

room, feeling like the unwanted dog at the feast. When she reached the kitchen she covered her embarrassment by marching toward the door with purpose.

Tiffany Wright and Bunny Fitzhugh were friends? She pondered this as she backed her truck around. It might have made sense if Tiffany were really related to William Montague, as she'd claimed, but Beau had already proven that untrue. Unless maybe . . . Tiffany might have convinced Bunny that she was a relative of Montague, while the two of them were an item. That didn't entirely wash either. Montague would have blown her cover immediately.

At the front of the house, two men in short monkey-jackets, inadequate for the chill weather, were seeing the guests out of their cars and valet parking them in an adjacent lot. Sam scanned the lot as she drove past but didn't spot any red Nissan sedans. As she negotiated the turns on the steep downhill road, she began to wonder whether she'd imagined the whole encounter just now. Bunny hadn't called the female guest by name—only her trademark 'darling!' And any number of women could have dark hair styled the same as Tiffany's.

She decided to banish the whole encounter from her thoughts as she approached the bakery. She'd left a huge mess of dirty bowls and utensils and it would be well past dinner time before she got the kitchen in decent shape for tomorrow's business.

As it turned out, she was elbow deep in suds when a tap came at the back door. Checking through the peephole, she saw that it was Beau.

"Saw your truck and thought I'd see how things were going," he said, wiping mud off his boots before entering.

Sam explained the nearly-forgotten order that would have landed her in big trouble, and the confusing near-encounter at Bunny Fitzhugh's home.

"It was probably just the fact that I was all keyed up over the cake delivery that I thought one of Bunny's guests was Tiffany Wright."

Beau picked up a dish towel and started drying the pieces Sam had already washed.

"I don't know what to tell you on that," he said. "This Montague guy seemed to be in the middle of a lot of things. I'm still trying to find out who Tiffany Wright is and what her connection is with that import company in Albuquerque. Mainly, I have to concentrate on finding Will Montague, now that his brother has turned up and we've *officially* started our investigation."

"Beau? What was your impression of Robert Montague?"

His forehead crinkled. "What do you mean?"

"I don't know exactly. I mean, he seemed sincere and all. It just seemed like . . . well, I got the impression something was just a little *off.*"

"I got identification from him. He willingly gave a DNA sample. How much more legit could the guy be?"

"Yeah, you're right. I think I'm just tired."

"You're working too hard these days," he said, edging toward her and ruffling her hair. "You need a vacation."

"Ha! Like that's going to happen right now. The very, *very* soonest might be sometime after New Year's day."

"Can I take that as a promise?"

"What do you have in mind?" She glanced sideways at him. "You mean you could actually get some time off from the department?"

He set the last of the clean decorating tips with the rest of the gear on the work table. "I don't know. Maybe."

Sam dried her hands and started storing the clean cake pans. The stack of unfilled orders caught her eye, an untidy pile she'd left on her desk while she was panicking over the cake for Bunny.

"Let's talk about it after Christmas, can we? I can't even think straight this week." She held up the bunched pages. "First thing, I need to sort these and get a better system in place. I'll have a heart attack if there's another mess-up like today's."

"Deal," he said. He hung the soppy dish towels over a rack and picked up his coat. "I need to run by and check on Mama again."

Sam felt a stab of guilt that she'd still not made time to visit Iris in the hospital. She promised to stop by before going home.

"I'll be glad to wait. Take you to dinner afterward." His voice sounded hopeful.

She raised the order sheets again. "It's going to take awhile."

"No problem." He kissed her with his usual warmth and she thanked him for his help and for being so understanding.

"Just in case I don't get there tonight before visiting hours are over, give Iris my love, okay?" She watched him drive off, barely registering that it was already completely dark out.

As it turned out, Sam got to the hospital five minutes before the close of visiting hours and found Iris sound asleep. Beau had gone, the nurse said, about fifteen minutes earlier. She stood by the old woman's bedside and watched her gentle breathing. Iris's hands lay folded across her chest and Sam reached down and lifted one of them. It was cool to the touch. Sam held the wrinkled hand between both of her own until warmth began to flow between them. She tucked that hand under the blanket and did the same with Iris's other hand.

Sam chided herself for being so completely wrapped up in her business and promised to be better about attending to friends and family. And that thought reminded her that she'd not mailed her parents a gift yet either. Sheesh. Life was just getting too busy.

* * *

Monday morning's alarm went off way too early for Sam, especially as she remembered the leisurely awakening and sumptuous breakfast with Beau on Sunday. She cruised through the pre-dawn streets, watching for icy patches, finding few. Secretly, she hoped for more snow in time for Christmas, but wanted it to hold off until business slowed down a little.

As the morning scones, tarts and muffins baked, Sam assembled a couple of gift boxes and gathered goodies she knew her father would love. Mom would nag at him for eating so much sugar, but she'd been known to relax her standards a little at the holidays. Sam pulled the assortment together and tied each box with a purple ribbon. A box of Bobul's custom chocolates topped the stack, and Sam found a big shipping box to handle it all.

By the time Bobul arrived at six-thirty, she'd taped and labeled the box and scheduled a pickup online with FedEx, who would get it to the family home in Texas in good shape and in time for everyone to enjoy. She felt a little guilty that she'd not actually shopped for gifts, but realistically, she couldn't think of anything they would enjoy more.

"Is last week of holidays," Bobul said as he laid out his chocolate molds. "Soon to be gone."

"It always seems that way, doesn't it? We work like mad to be ready, then it's over so quickly," Sam said. From the look on his face, she wondered if he understood half of what she'd said. She turned to her newly organized filing system and pulled out the orders for the day.

Kelly arrived in time to take the freshly baked breakfast pastries out to the display cases, and Sam concentrated on cakes and cookies for the next few hours. She was just finishing a dozen cookie trays, tying bows around them when Beau called. She explained about their near-miss at the hospital the night before and promised to get there around midday.

"I hope your mom is allowed to have cookies?" she said. She remembered how Iris always lit up at the sight of goodies from the shop.

Beau assured her that Iris would love the gift and said that he would try to be there when Sam went to visit.

"Mainly what I called about was to let you know that we got some interesting information on that Global Imports Company. The state corporation commission shows Larry Lissano and Bunny Fitzhugh as owners."

"What? Surely not. It was a very bitter divorce, according to Rupert," she said. "I can't imagine them staying in business together."

"Just letting you know what the paperwork says. No guarantee that it's accurate, I guess."

Sam couldn't help brooding about the information while she worked. What was Larry Lissano doing with a business in Albuquerque anyway? He lived in Dallas. And Bunny seemed financially set for life from her settlement—she certainly didn't need a business in order to support herself, if Rupert's stories were true. Tiffany Wright—where did she come into the picture? The thought niggled at her brain that the business somehow provided that missing connection between Bunny and Tiffany, but Sam couldn't imagine what it would be. And imports? What were they importing? She pictured furniture from Mexico or rugs from India or some such thing, but none of it made sense.

She filled and frosted layers for a caroling party cake and set it into the fridge. Becky had created small figurines in chocolate for the carolers on Friday, and it would be a quick matter to make sugar cone pine trees. Sam formed a couple of lampposts and dusted the globes with luster powder to make them glow with light.

"I'll leave these here to firm up a bit, then I can put the whole thing together when I get back from the hospital," she told Kelly. "Can you hold down the fort if I stay away long enough to visit Iris and grab some lunch?"

Kelly gave one of those smiles that daughters give moms who underestimate them.

"Okay, I know you can. See you soon," Sam said, picking up Iris's cookie gift and heading out the back door.

There was something about walking into a hospital room that always gave Sam a twinge. Maybe it was because her mother did it so much; visiting the sick was such a part of west Texas culture and church life, a part that Sam never got comfortable with. Maybe it was just the sound of floors so clean they squeaked when you walked on them, the smell of disinfectants and medicines, the sight of people lying in beds exposed to view by all who passed down the hall. Aside from giving birth to Kelly thirty-four years ago, Sam had never been a patient so maybe it was the lack of exposure and conditioning that sent that gurgle into her stomach. Maybe she just needed some lunch.

Beau was standing at his mother's bedside when Sam entered the room. The sight of him in uniform never failed to catch her attention, and it seemed the same for Iris's roommate, a woman of about ninety whose bug-eyed stare was clearly making Beau uncomfortable.

"Hi, Iris," Sam said, ignoring the infatuated roommate and approaching Beau's side. "Well, I have to say that you look really good."

Better than she'd expected. Iris smiled a little lopsidedly but she reached both arms toward Sam for a hug. When she spoke it was only with a faint slur.

"I feel pretty good, too, honey. Pretty good."

"The nurse tells us that Mama is moving to the rehab place in the morning. That's a lot better than we expected at this point."

The roommate looked a little saddened by this news, probably because she wouldn't be able to ogle Beau any more.

"Well, Iris, that's great news." Sam set the cookie tray on Iris's lap. "They might want you to wait until you've had your lunch before you get into these, but I won't tell."

The spark was still in the elderly woman's eye as she

tugged at the ribbon and loosened the cellophane enough to help herself to an almond crescent coated in powdered sugar. As his mother munched on her cookie, Beau offered one to the roommate. She took her time in deciding but he was finally able to pull away and set the gift safely on Iris's nightstand.

They talked for another fifteen minutes before the lunch trays showed up, then Beau helped Iris with her meal. She still wasn't quite good enough with the utensils to get the food to her mouth every time, but Sam supposed that was what rehab was all about.

Iris's eyes began to droop within minutes after removal of the lunch tray, so they tucked the blanket around her shoulders and left her to her afternoon nap.

"I'm happy to see her doing so well," Sam said, as she and Beau walked toward the parking lot.

"I'm relieved," he said. "Things could have gone a whole lot worse. Makes you realize how short life can be. And how bad hospital food can be. Let's go somewhere decent for lunch."

"Before that, since we're pretty close to Talpa, would you mind if we ran that box of files back out to the Montague place? I'd like to be rid of that responsibility."

He agreed and they made the short drive in Sam's truck. They were halfway up the flagstone walk when they heard a vehicle on the road. A dark blue SUV parked and Robert Montague got out.

Chapter 24

I'm glad you stopped by," Beau said, shaking hands with the military-straight Montague. "Remember that we talked about your brother's bank records?"

They walked around the house and entered through the French doors at the back. Sam placed the heavy box of files on the kitchen counter while she attended to the sign-in sheet. She felt a nervous energy from Robert as Beau spoke to him.

"I ran a search on William's bank records and I'm afraid there's been no activity in the past three months. I guess that's good news and bad news. At least no one has hijacked his accounts and cleaned them out."

Rob Montague walked through the living room and into the kitchen, his gaze taking in the art and furnishings. "Yes

. . . I suppose that's good news. But Will would be making withdrawals to live on. If he were alive."

"We're doing all we can to find out. My men were at the property over the weekend, searching with a canine team. They found nothing, well, no evidence of a death."

"That's only slightly reassuring."

"I know. We just have very few leads to go on. His phone records essentially went blank after September."

"It doesn't sound good then, does it?" Rob's tone was matter-of-fact.

Beau leaned against the granite bar, facing Rob who stood near the refrigerator. "You indicated that you didn't want your brother's property to go into foreclosure. We've discovered that there is enough in his various accounts to cover about half the amount owed in back mortgage payments." He turned to Sam.

"I spoke with my contracting officer at the USDA," she said. "He furnished the figures. He can arrange to release the lien on the property if you will sign some paperwork for him. He also said to remind you that the payments would need to be kept current or the same thing will happen again."

Rob stared at the floor, chewing at the side of his cheek.

Sam handed him a business card for Delbert Crow. "I'll just put these files back in the desk and I can get the banking information for you."

He started to say something but when she turned toward him, he remained silent.

She went into Montague's study and replaced all the files except the one with the bank statements. Something about this whole thing still felt strange but she really couldn't define it. She glanced toward the bookcases—that wasn't it. These particular vibes were coming from Robert Montague, not from this house.

When she touched the center drawer of the desk a vision of her wooden box came to her. She hadn't touched it in a few days. What if she had? Would she be getting even stronger impressions from Rob Montague?

She tried to shed the feeling but it wouldn't go away. Sometimes she would see auras, get waves of emotional signals from other people after handling the box. Maybe she should start doing that again, start using its influence to help Beau with this case.

She picked up the banking file and a checkbook that she'd found in one of the drawers and walked back to the kitchen. The men were gone but she could hear their voices from the direction of the master bedroom.

Rob stood over the spot where they'd found the blood. Sam stopped dead in the doorway. A humming sound drummed at her ears and her vision went wavy. Then it stopped. Just like that.

She gripped the doorjamb for support and closed her eyes.

"Sam? Are you all right, darlin'?"

When she opened her eyes Beau stood near her. Even Rob looked a little concerned.

"Yeah . . . I'm fine. I guess I just had a little dizzy spell."

"I better get you some lunch." Beau took her elbow and led her toward the back door.

"I can lock up here," Robert Montague said, reaching out for the key.

Sam felt her energy return. "Sorry, I can't give you

these until my supervisor releases me from the job." She shrugged. "Government policy."

A muscle worked in his jaw but he didn't say anything. He followed them outside and both men waited while Sam locked the door. Montague's nervous energy seemed stronger than ever as they walked out to the vehicles. Sam fiddled with her keys and backpack, stalling so Rob would drive away before she did.

"What is with these people?" she demanded as she cranked the pickup to life. "Everybody wants the keys to this place, no matter what I tell them about the rules."

"You don't trust that Rob is who he says he is?" Beau regarded her from the corner of his eye. "Sam, are you getting another of those . . . whatever you call 'em . . . visions?"

She blew out a breath. "I don't know. It's nothing definite. Maybe it's just me."

"I noticed he got quiet when we were talking about him keeping up the payments on the house. Maybe it's more than he can afford?"

Turning left onto 585, she concentrated on traffic for a minute. "It's not just him, Beau. It's Tiffany. It's everyone who comes out of the woodwork as a former friend of William Montague. They all want something."

"The million dollars worth of art that's in that house, maybe?"

When he said it like that, it was kind of a *duh* revelation. Of course anyone would want to lay claim to the art. But now there was verifiable proof that the art didn't belong to Montague, and therefore not to any of his family. They'd never win that argument in court.

Unless they didn't intend to go to court. Possession was

nine-tenths of the law—or something like that.

Then it hit her. Maybe it wasn't the art at all. Maybe it was the contents of the secret room.

When Rob's eyes had scanned the entire house, just now, maybe he wasn't looking at what he could easily see. Maybe he was looking for the odd assortment of collectibles, those macabre bones and tools and that godawful green robe. And since they weren't readily apparent, perhaps he even knew that there would be a hidden switch, a way into the place where the cache lay concealed.

She voiced those thoughts to Beau.

"Really? You think that weird junk is worth a lot?" Clearly, he wouldn't have given two dollars for the whole lot.

"Well . . . I don't know." She felt a little helpless in the face of his logic. How did one explain a sensation of the supernatural to a regular, sensible, no-nonsense man who dealt everyday in facts and evidence? It was pretty hopeless.

She changed the subject and they decided to grab fast food for lunch, since both of them had been away from business longer than they'd planned. By the time they'd scarfed some fried chicken and she'd taken Beau back to the hospital lot to retrieve his cruiser, she was feeling behind the gun again with bakery orders.

A running list of party cakes and wedding cakes and specialty items kept her mind going non-stop as she drove toward her little shop a block off the plaza. When she walked in the back door, Bobul gave her a hard look.

"Miss Sam running from dark force," he said.

She laughed. "I'm running, all right."

She washed her hands and started again on the caroling

party cake, which was due to be picked up at four o'clock. As she placed the chocolate figurines and piped green royal icing on sugar cones to make pine trees, she noticed that Bobul kept sneaking sidelong glances at her. But she didn't have time to think much about it.

When the customer came for the caroler cake, Sam carried it out front herself, proud to show how well it had turned out. Everyone in the shop exclaimed over the scene, with its snowbanks, lampposts, and the half-dozen carolers in traditional Victorian clothing. Two more customers placed orders on the spot. Sam smiled and secretly wondered if she was going to live through this first season.

* * *

Kelly put an arm around Sam's shoulders as Jen switched off the daytime lights, leaving only a lamp and the strings of holiday lights at the windows for ambiance. Everyone felt beat, and they still had six days to go.

"Next year, I'll get a few more part-time helpers," Sam said. "Kel, I don't know what I'd be doing right now without you."

This time the daughter-smile was genuinely pleased.

"Do you mind if I skip out on dinner at home tonight, Mom? I actually have a movie date."

"Oooh, a date," Sam teased. "I'll bet you're asleep in your seat before the second scene."

"It's action-adventure. A real guy-thing. So, yeah, I probably will be."

The two younger women left and Sam gave the counter and tables a final wipe-down before going back to see what kind of shape the kitchen was in. Bobul's molds were clean and sitting neatly on the worktable, ready to accept more batches of chocolate tomorrow. She eyed the supply of gift boxes, which was running low, but decided against ordering more. They would probably run out by Christmas Eve, but that was okay. The demand for the chocolates gratified her and she looked forward to seeing what new confections Bobul would create once the winter holidays were over.

The chocolatier stood at the sink, swishing a chocolate coated bowl in sudsy water. It appeared to be almost the last of the dirty dishes. When he became aware of Sam's presence, he gave her the same look he'd been sending her way all afternoon.

"Bobul, what is it? Do I have some gory red frosting mark on my face?"

She bit back her impatience and realized that he probably didn't understand the sarcasm anyway. "Sorry. It's just—is there something you want to say to me?"

He dried his hands on a towel as he turned to face her. "Miss Sam in danger."

That wasn't at all what she expected.

"Danger? What kind of danger, Bobul?" His earlier remark about her running from a dark force came back and a chill went up her arms.

"The man. Man you cannot find. He want the box. Facinor. He try very hard to get Facinor because evil woman want it."

The damn box again. Sam felt like she was reaching her wits end with this stuff.

"Evil woman is having connection to *bruja*. She want to be new Lorena."

"You told me about Lorena, Bobul, but you said she died many years ago."

He stepped forward and placed his hands on the worktable, tracing a pattern with a fingertip, as if he were drawing a lesson picture for a rather slow child.

"Old Lorena dead. New Lorena will come. New Lorena use Facinor for evil plans."

What evil plans? she wanted to demand. "Bobul, how does this put me in danger? I don't know any Lorena. Or any *bruja* at all, for that matter."

He gave her a piercing look and she had the sense that he knew something about her possession of the wooden box and the fact that Bertha Martinez had given it to her. But she'd never told him. Maybe it was the photo of the box that concerned him. She unzipped her pack and pulled out the picture.

"Is it this, Bobul? Is this *picture* what's making you so worried?"

He stared, not taking his gaze from it.

"Okay. Fine. Look, we can easily get rid of this," she said. She walked over to the stove and lit a burner.

Her voice rose, shaking. "We don't have to let the picture of the box—*Facinor*, if you will—we don't *have* to let it scare us." She dipped a corner of the photo into the flame and let it catch. As the fire raced across the thick paper, she carried it to the sink and just before it would have touched her fingers, she dropped it into the dishwater.

"There. See? Gone." She raised her empty hands to show him.

"Bobul not stupid, Miss Sam. Burning picture not to getting rid of box. Burning old Lorena not be rid of box. You do not understanding."

She sighed. "I guess I don't. It's okay. Why don't you go on home."

He kept his eyes on her as he edged toward the coat hooks and reached for his massive rough brown one. He shoved his arms into the sleeves and buttoned the front. "Please, Miss Sam be careful. There is a woman. She will harm Miss." He gave an almost regretful stare and then turned and walked out the back door.

Chapter 25

What did he mean by that? Sam wondered, rubbing the chill away from her arms. She strode over to the door and flung it open, ready to confront Bobul for more details, but he was gone.

She locked the metal door and stood with her back to it. *Okay, Sam. Let's think rationally and see if we can figure this out.* But at the moment she couldn't think at all.

She scrubbed the two remaining mixing bowls in the sink, drained the water, took tomorrow's orders out of the file and laid them on the worktable where she would see them immediately in the morning. Quick movements, deliberate actions—they were her defense against insanity at the moment.

I will not think about this. There is no evil woman. There is no evil in that stupid wooden box. There is not any *power*— But she had to stop. The box did have power. Sam could no more explain it than she could describe quantum physics, but she couldn't deny the box's power. She'd experienced it too many times.

Okay, she thought, pulling on her jacket, *if someone else wants the stupid box let them have it. I'll just get rid of it. The damn thing has caused me nothing but grief anyway.* She snatched up her pack and headed out the door.

Her hands felt shaky on the wheel and she had to force herself to breathe evenly and drive carefully. Puddled water made icy patches on the roads, now that it was dark. But as she got closer to home, determination took over. She whipped into her driveway and hit the brakes at the last second. She left the truck running and dashed into the house, switching on lights as she raced to her bedroom.

The box lay under the scarf, just as she'd left it. She grabbed it up without looking closely at it, opened the lid and dumped her few pieces of jewelry onto the bed. She carried it back to the truck and gunned the accelerator the whole length of the driveway.

The landfill was clear across town but Sam was determined to rid herself once and for all of the curse of the box. She headed that direction, her new confidence in the mission providing the right amount of caution in her driving. But when she got there, the gates were closed. The posted hours stated that they opened at eight in the morning. And there was a warning in red that there was absolutely no dumping outside the fence.

To hell with that. She stepped back, balanced the box in the palm of her hand, and wound up for the throw. With all her strength she flung the wooden box over the fence. She jumped back into her truck, hit the gas and got the heck out of there.

Okay. Done. My life will settle down quite nicely now. But before she reached home tears began to prickle at her eyes. Apart from all the silly nonsense Bobul had rattled, the box had been a gift from Bertha Martinez. And it had introduced Sam to something deep inside herself. Something she'd never desired, never even considered, but she had in fact helped people with the powers from the box.

"Oh, don't be a ninny," she said as she got out of the truck and stomped into her kitchen. "You never wanted those powers and it's better that you get back to your *real* life."

She shed her coat, took a shower, and found a frozen low-cal dinner that she microwaved and ate, sitting alone at her table. She scooped the jewelry off the bed and left it in a glittery little pile on the dresser top, then crawled between the sheets and closed her eyes, ready for a solid night's sleep.

At some point she heard small sounds—Kelly coming in from her movie date—but her next conscious act was to shut off her alarm when it rang at four-thirty.

In her usual early-morning blur, Sam got into her bakers jacket and black pants, washed her face and brushed her teeth. Her short, gray-threaded hair stuck out wildly and even dampening and blow drying didn't make a lot of difference. She scowled at the dark circles under her eyes and put on an extra swipe of lipstick to make up for it.

Coffee. She just needed her morning coffee at the bakery.

Her winter coat wasn't on its normal hook near the door so she wandered back into the bedroom. The middle of her dresser caught her eye. The pile of jewelry she'd placed there last night was gone. And smack in the middle of the dresser top sat the wooden box.

The carved surface and dull yellowish varnish were unmistakable. The cabochon stones of red, green and blue, mounted in the cross-hatches of the quilted design, were dark and unhappy. Sam's heart thudded heavily and rapidly.

No, no, no-no-no . . . She backed away from the dresser.

"Kelly! Kelly!" Sam ran toward her daughter's room and twisted the doorknob. "Did you set that box on my dresser?"

Kelly sat up in bed, looking like a mole who'd been yanked suddenly out of hibernation. She blinked at the light from the hall. "What?"

"My jewelry box. Did you find it somewhere and put it on my dresser?" Sam worked to keep her voice from sounding as panicky as it felt.

"No, Mom. I don't know what you mean."

Sam backed away. "It's okay. Ignore me." She rubbed at her temples. "Kel, what time did you get home last night?"

"Um, maybe around eleven?"

"And everything looked okay? The door was locked and all?"

"Yeah . . . Mom, you're kind of scaring me."

Sam forced a normal expression onto her face. "It's okay. I guess I just misplaced something . . ."

She closed Kelly's door and walked toward her room. The box still sat there.

Sam walked over and touched it. Nothing happened. She lifted the lid and saw her jewelry inside, not neatly laid out as she would normally leave it, but heaped in a pile of chains and earrings, as if someone had scooped it off the edge of the dresser and into the box. But when? Had she slept so soundly that someone could have come into her room?

No. She was a mom. She was not *that* heavy a sleeper.

She glanced at the clock and realized that she needed to be on her way. She would need every spare moment of this day at Sweet's Sweets.

Her mind reeled as she drove the few blocks to the pastry shop. Yes, life had gotten a bit frantic these days, but not so crazy that she would make up something like this. Maybe she'd only dreamed the part about going to the dump and discarding the box. Not unless she were going insane. The container from her frozen dinner was still in the trash—she'd eaten that *after* getting rid of the wooden box. And she hadn't imagined the crisp tire tracks where she'd pulled in after work and then left for the dump last night. She wanted to laugh insanely, and cry, and check herself into the loony bin.

She parked behind the bakery and sat in the truck for at least ten minutes, letting the cold seep into her bones and wake her up.

Somehow, Sam, you've got to pull yourself through this.

Chapter 26

The unbelievable events of the night faded, once Sam began studying the bake shop's orders for the day. She had a wedding cake and two large party cakes to make and deliver, in addition to the usual fare for the customers who walked in the door.

While Sam was inside the walk-in, finding the big box of roses Becky had made for the bride's cake—peach and ivory to go over a creamy fondant—Bobul arrived and went right to his work. It startled Sam to see him there—he tended to move about like a ghost. He gave her a cryptic look and neither of them brought up the conversation from the previous evening.

The wedding cake was glamorous but deceptively simple. Vanilla cake draped in ivory fondant, smoothed and trimmed, then completely covered in the roses. Those, being made from sugar paste, had been done days ago and now all Sam had to do was fit them in a solid mass over the entire three tiers. She had it finished and stashed outside in the delivery van by eight o'clock.

When Becky called a few minutes later, saying that her mother-in-law was in town all week and would love to watch the boys, did Sam need help at the bakery, she almost wept with relief. Yes, absolutely. She didn't realize how much she'd missed her right-hand assistant the past few days.

By ten, the breakfast crowd had waned and as Sam worked on the party cakes, Becky and Kelly turned out dozens of cookies, pies and cupcakes. Kelly was getting better all the time at making the batters without mixing them up—no more chocolate into the carrot cakes. And Becky swore she was glad to be piping Santa faces rather than dealing with kids who were bored three days into their winter vacation.

Sam let Bobul and the girls work in their own little worlds while she concentrated on the sheet cakes. One was for a construction business's open-house, so she duplicated the company logo in fondant, then made walls of a house out of gingerbread and set them up with molded chocolate two-by-fours so it looked like it was under construction. Crushed cookies formed the raw earth around the project and she even found enough of the moldable candy to make a miniature cement mixer, from which poured a gray sidewalk of icing.

The second cake didn't get quite so much attention, unfortunately, because the phone rang just as she was getting it started.

Delbert Crow needed her to get out to the Montague

place at one o'clock to meet with Robert, who had covered the back payments and was now entitled to have the keys to his brother's house. He said he'd emailed some forms for her to print out and have Robert sign.

Sam sighed and looked around the busy kitchen. She could deliver the wedding cake any time, and probably the sooner the better. The construction cake was going to an office on the south end of town, so it would be on her way to the Montague place. She called Becky over and showed her the plans for the other sheet cake.

"If you'll fill and ice it," Sam said, "and get the poinsettias made, I'll do the piping when I get back."

Becky gave her a little thumbs-up. It was good to have her back, and smiling.

With the two cakes safely delivered by noon, Sam debated whether to go back to the bakery or just head out to Montague's. There and back through traffic would eat up forty minutes of the hour, so there didn't seem much point in heading back to the center of town. Plus, it would probably be smart of her to re-check the house one more time, in case there were things she needed to review with Robert Montague before she officially quit her caretaking duties there.

Sunday's early snowfall hadn't quite melted off in the shady places and she noticed a somewhat fresh set of tire tracks that swerved in close to Montague's perimeter wall, seemed to stop there, then pulled away to the east. A car sat at the end of those tracks, about a hundred yards beyond the property line. Someone heading for the neighbor's place got the wrong address on the first try.

Sam parked in her usual spot near the mailbox and walked through the gateway. Around back, she let herself into the living room and headed for the study. A half-second before she stepped into the room, she heard a sound. Paper rustling. Then a low female voice. She flattened herself against the wall, listening. Muted sounds of a drawer opening.

She should run. She should call Beau. She knew that.

But whoever it was might get away before he could get here. She had to find out who was sneaking around in William Montague's study. She risked a peek around the doorsill.

Tiffany Wright and Bunny Fitzhugh were at the desk, a cascade of files and papers littering the top.

"I don't see any code here, or a safe deposit key or anything," Tiffany said.

"Well, then there's a name. He had a picture of the box so he must have found the owner. He—" Bunny glanced up at the door and spotted Sam.

"What on earth are you doing?" Sam demanded, not giving the wealthy woman a chance to put her on the defensive. She stepped into the doorway, hands on hips.

"I might ask you the same thing," Bunny said. But her voice had a slight waver to it.

"I'm here as legal caretaker for the property, and I'm meeting the rightful owner in—" She meant to say that Robert Montague would be along any minute, but Tiffany slammed the center drawer of the desk and both women charged at Sam.

She probably outweighed the two of them and could easily block their exit, but her attention was drawn to the wall behind them. The bookcase was slowly swinging outward. Sam stepped aside to let the would-be thieves dash out of the room, then she moved over and closed the door.

Down the hall, Tiffany and Bunny were making a mad

dash for the front hall. A shriek got her attention and she headed that direction. When Sam turned the corner in the hall, the women were jammed up against the military presence of Robert Montague.

He was staring at Bunny with a hard glare.

"They were going through Will's desk," Sam said.

"Did they take anything?"

"I don't think so. I caught them going through files."

Bunny raised her chin proudly. "Will and I were very close. I believe that he had something that belongs to me."

"Ahem, I don't think so," Sam interjected. "The conversation I overheard was more about something you wanted him to acquire for you. A piece of art, maybe?"

"Get out of here," Robert said to Bunny. "This is my property now and I don't want to see you here, ever again."

He stepped out of the way so the women had access to the front door.

Sam caught Bunny's expression as she edged past him. Her chiseled features were drawn into an expression of pure malevolence. She continued giving him the evil eye until she and Tiffany had crossed the hall and gone out onto the front porch.

Robert walked over to the windows and watched until they had left. "One of them had a key," he said. "The door was unlocked when I got here."

"I'm sorry I didn't notice it," Sam said. "I could have called the sheriff."

"It's probably better that you caught them in the act and scared them off."

Robert's edginess from their previous meetings seemed to be gone. He pulled out a PDA. "Making a note to get the locks changed," he said.

As Sam walked back down the hall, her thoughts drifted elsewhere. She'd always believed that Tiffany, miffed at not getting Sam to let her in the house, had hammered at the lockbox and damaged the front door. But what if she and Bunny had been in cahoots all along? Bunny must have had a key, and she'd come once before, going through the desk, looking for the photo or the box itself. While Tiffany's interest was in the art, Bunny wanted the power of the box. One or both of them, whoever was here that day, must have heard Sam arrive and ducked around the side of the house to get away. She shuddered at the close call.

"If you ask me," Rob said, "I don't think Bunny is actually dangerous. I think that it's her ex, Larry Lissano, who killed my brother."

Sam glanced over her shoulder at him and didn't voice her own thoughts.

"There was really that much animosity between Lissano and Will?"

"Bunny might like to pretend that the affair was nothing, that it was over a long time ago, but Lissano was furious. And he's the kind of man who doesn't let go of things. When Will told me about some threats he received, I did a little checking into the guy. That import company of his— nothing but a front for dealing arms and drugs. Feds have been after him for a long time but they can't seem to find enough to take it to trial."

"Seriously? You think Lissano would risk committing murder, knowing the authorities are watching him that closely?"

"Lissano deals with some of the roughest characters on the planet. Arms deals to rogue nations, paying off dictators to help huge drug deals get past the DEA. He might not have pulled the trigger, or whatever happened, but he sure as hell was behind it."

Sam straightened her shoulders. Maybe this was why she'd gotten strange vibes around Rob. He knew a lot about his brother's enemies, information he hadn't shared with Beau. The sooner she could be done with this place and all the wackos associated with it, the better.

"Shall we go over the paperwork?" She steered him toward the kitchen, wondering whether to break the news about the hidden room or just let him stumble in there and let that ugly green robe scare the pants off him, like it had done to her.

She pulled out the forms Delbert Crow had sent and began to read over the paragraphs that would transfer responsibility for the care and expenses on the property to him, the surviving brother. She'd just flipped to the second page where his signature was required, when Rob looked up. His face blanched and he suddenly looked unsteady on his feet.

"Oh. My. God." He stared with wide eyes at a figure who stepped out of the woods and was heading across the lawn. "Will."

Chapter 27

Sam's attention became riveted. The man was not as tall as his brother, nor as straight in stature. In fact, he almost shuffled across the brown winter lawn. His clothing fit sloppily and his hair was quite a lot longer than he wore it in the old pictures. Several days' worth of beard darkened his jawline.

"That's your brother?" she started to ask. But Rob Montague was on his way out the door.

He ran toward the other man, who stopped, looked up and then started to crumple. Rob grabbed him by the shoulders and helped steady him. Together, they stumbled toward the house. Sam pulled a tumbler from a cabinet and drew a glass of cold tap water for him.

Rob was talking almost non-stop as the men came back

inside, but Will seemed drained of even the basic energy to speak. He sank onto one of the leather couches and Sam handed him the water. He drank greedily and cleared his throat, staring at her with a puzzled expression.

She introduced herself with a brief explanation of why she was in his home, before she carried the empty glass back to the kitchen.

"—can't stay here alone," Rob was saying when Sam came back.

"I'll do what I need to," Will insisted. "Just go."

Rob looked like he meant to argue, but a glare from older brother shut him down. "I'll be at the La Fonda, and I plan to stay in town until I know you're all right."

"I'm all right. Go back to California." Will stood up and started for the kitchen. "I'm hungry."

Sam spoke up. "Sorry, Mr. Montague, but the food in the fridge was all spoiled. I threw everything out."

He'd reached the cupboards and began rummaging through them, coming up with a can of baked beans and a waxed-paper tube of saltine crackers. "This'll do me."

Sam glanced at the photos on the mantle again. The smiling Will Montague in a tuxedo holding a flute of champagne was a far cry from the emaciated man in filthy clothing who stood at the kitchen counter, spooning cold beans from a can.

Rob had watched the desperation on his brother's face but gave up trying to make suggestions. He sent Sam a penetrating look, mimed "let me know" and left.

"There's some paperwork," Sam said. "Your brother got the past due bills caught up and was about to sign these so I could release the house to him. I guess you'll want to do that now."

Will glanced at the pages, his mouth bulging with food. He swallowed and refilled the water glass. "I don't know how long I can stay," he said, his voice quiet with fatigue. "Someone tried to kill me. Maybe you already know that."

"Actually, we thought they had killed you," Sam said. "The sheriff is investigating. I should call him so he can get your statement."

"No!" Will moved toward her. "If people think I'm dead, maybe that's good."

"Why? Don't you want your friends to know you're okay? Don't you want to resume your art business?"

He looked as if he'd already considered this. "Friends and business will just have to wait. I can't afford to be seen. Not yet."

"Tell me what happened."

He stuffed another spoonful of the beans into his mouth, still sizing her up, gauging whether he could trust her.

"I accidentally found your secret room," she said. "And a photograph of a strange wooden box."

Montague choked. He spat the beans into the sink and struggled for a few seconds.

"You might as well tell me. I know something about that box. Why did you have a picture of it?"

"A client. I was commissioned to find it for her."

"Does it have anything to do with the, uh, unorthodox collection in the hidden room?"

"Ah, well, that room," he said after he'd taken a long drink of water. "I discovered it when I bought the house. Some of the old, outdated medical instruments and books were in it. I began to read them and that got me started, looking for other oddities. Over the years I collected a lot of the old dental tools and such."

Including bones? Okay. Weird hobby.

"That dark green robe—is that something to do with medicine as well?" The very thought made her stomach clench up.

"It was here too. I can't tell you how many times I've reached for it, thinking I would throw it out. But something always stopped me, some kind of force seems to surround the thing. I finally found a collector who wanted it. I was about to be rid of the bizarre thing once and for all."

Thank goodness he had some kind of creep-limits.

"I was supposed to deliver it the next day—the next day after September twenty-fourth." He rubbed his hands down the sides of his face. "I can't believe I've been away this long."

"What happened here? What sent you on the run?"

He dropped the empty bean can into the trash and filled his water glass for the third time. Sam followed him into the living room where he flopped into an easy chair.

"I feel like I've been walking forever. There was never a comfortable place to sit down." He took a deep breath. "It was late September, business as usual. I'm working at my desk and hear a noise in my bedroom. Went to check on it. Two huge goons jumped me. I kept a baseball bat under my desk and thank goodness I thought to pick it up before I went in there. Smashed one of them in the head. He went down but the other one came after me. I ran out. Got out to the woods—it was dark. Guess I only got away because I was smaller and lighter and knew my way around out there."

"The sheriff found blood in the bedroom and a broken vase."

"Yeah, that got knocked off the nightstand. Guy I hit, probably his blood."

"The other guy must have come back and taken his buddy away," Sam guessed.

Montague shrugged. "Guess so. I sneaked back in for my computer but there wasn't time to take much of anything. Had my wallet in my pocket but I got scared to use credit cards or bank accounts. I took the max from the first ATM I came to, that same night. That, plus a pretty good cash commission from a client . . . that's what I've been living on. Slept in sheds, sprang for a really cheap motel now and then."

"So, why didn't you just report it? They invaded your *home*. They would have been arrested."

Montague snorted. "You don't get it, do you? These were Larry Lissano's men."

Sam felt like the kid who'd not read the assigned chapter. "Lissano would hold a grudge for years? What was his problem with you?"

"Aside from the very stupid affair I had with his wife, I can't think of much."

"But they've been divorced for awhile. From what I gathered, he would have been a lot more angry with her than with you." Bunny was the one who took her ex for a fortune.

"I said they were Lissano's men. I didn't say he sent them."

Huh? Sam was wading in deep mud here.

"I think Bunny sent them."

"And that would be because . . .?"

He glanced around, clearly unsure how much to tell her.

"The wooden box. Bunny was the client. That woman is obsessed. She wants that box, no matter what the cost. Okay, so I don't know anything about the box—to me it's an artifact of some kind. She seems to think it has some kind of powers and that she's the one person in the whole world who is somehow *destined* to own this box. Whatever. I told her I'd try to locate it. The damn thing is supposedly famous. It has a name and everything. Facin—something— I don't know. So I have a photo of this box, I've learned that some old woman here in Taos owned it, I tell Bunny I'm pretty close to finding it for her."

Sam held very still, forcing her facial expression not to reveal anything.

"You think she'd be grateful. You'd think she'd be all over me with sweet talk and lovey-dovey. No. Bunny comes all unglued, starts calling me day and night, pestering, 'where's the box, where's the box?' until I'm about to go nuts. Then she goes completely paranoid. Starts to think I've got the box and I'm just not giving it to her. That's when the goons show up."

"And you're pretty sure Bunny sent them to force the information out of you?"

"I believe so. The woman is truly evil."

Sam's mouth twitched. Montague broke into a smile. "Yeah, I know. An evil bunny—" He broke into a laugh that lasted about two seconds. "Don't underestimate her, Ms Sweet. Seriously, she's off her rocker."

"I'm surprised the two men didn't ransack the place, trying to find the box."

"Me too. If they walked into my study they would have seen a photograph of it and my notes about the search. I didn't have names yet, any contacts for locating it, and the notes clearly showed that I hadn't found it yet. The guy who was still standing could have just grabbed up the notes for Bunny and then decided he better get his buddy to a doctor." He shrugged.

Sam puzzled over that for a minute. The guy probably had grabbed the notes and given them to Bunny. Otherwise, this house would have been a shambles when Sam got assigned to it. Somehow, though, he'd missed the photograph in the drawer. Bunny may have recently found another dealer she could trust and that's why she'd come back twice, looking for the photo of the box.

Sam told Will about walking into the house earlier and finding Tiffany and Bunny going through his desk. "One of them must have hit the switch to the secret room, because that door started to swing open."

"Oh, god, did she see it?"

"No. Luckily, I was facing the bookcases—they were facing the door and I got them out of the study. Rob made them leave when he showed up."

"She won't give up."

"Do you want protection from the sheriff's department?"

"It won't do any good. She'll either come back herself or she'll hire those huge guys to catch me in a dark alley somewhere. I have to stay out of sight until . . . I don't know."

He sounded so discouraged that Sam felt sorry for him. It would be hard to live that way, hiding and knowing someone was after you.

"We have to at least tell the sheriff that you are alive and well. There's an open investigation into your disappearance and probable death, right now."

He stood up and paced the room. "I don't like it."

"Will, no one *likes* it. But Beau Cardwell is smart and he'll be discreet."

He thought about it for two or three minutes before he turned to her. "I guess. Call him."

She did, and Beau agreed to come alone and not to say anything within the department.

An hour later the three of them were sitting at Montague's dining table. He'd repeated the whole story to Beau, who took careful notes and got descriptions of the two attackers. He promised to quietly close the missing person's case without fanfare, then he asked Montague if he wanted to press charges against Bunny Fitzhugh or Tiffany Wright for breaking and entering.

"No, I can't risk it. If she knows I'm alive—"

"Sam could actually be the witness who files the report. She arrived here today, found the two women in your home. The open front door and fingerprints which are surely all over the files provide plenty of evidence."

"And what would I gain?" Will said. "Even if they took something, which Sam says they didn't, all I get is unwanted publicity. Bunny might, at most, get a slap-on-the-wrist judgment against her, which would infuriate her."

"Beau, I think he's right," Sam said. "Bunny doesn't need one more reason to be angry at Will."

Beau and Sam left the worried homeowner with a warning about keeping drapes closed and having a watchful eye. Beau gave him both the department numbers and his own direct line.

Sam glanced uneasily at the house as she pulled away. Montague's recount of the details about the wooden box were an uncanny match for what Bobul had told her, and she didn't for one minute believe that Bunny wouldn't try again for the box.

Chapter 28

Sam was a half-mile from her house when the phone rang. She'd decided to go home, get the box, and take it somewhere for safe keeping. It seemed like a pain to rent a safe-deposit box at the bank, but it was the only thing she could think of at the moment. The cell call, however, changed all that.

"Mom, we've got a little bakery emergency here," Kelly said. "A lady swears she placed an order for a birthday cake—" she lowered her voice "—for Jesus. Uh, yeah. And we can't find either the order or the cake."

"I think that's one I would remember," Sam said. "The lady is mistaken, but if you want to keep her there, I can swing by and we'll see what we can do."

Sheesh. Would the drama of this day never end?

By the time Sam entered the bakery through the back door, Jen, in her most diplomatic way, had coaxed the information that the cake was to be chocolate, the frosting vanilla buttercream and the design was to include a manger-type crib with a baby in it.

"We can manage," Sam said. "There are some chocolate layers in the fridge that weren't committed to anyone else. Buttercream, we have by the tubs. Offer the woman a pastry and some coffee and just keep visiting with her."

She reached for her apron and began assembling ingredients. "Becky, can you fill and ice this and pipe a shell border on it? I'll see whether I can manage to make a baby that doesn't look too deformed."

Becky chuckled and started in with the cake.

"Miss Sam, Bobul help."

She'd walked right past the chocolatier without noticing what he was doing.

"I hear ladies talking," he said. "Here is baby." He held up a perfectly sculpted infant, with a blanket draped over its midsection. The skintone was probably a little pale, but hey, this was winter, and Sam thought it looked great anyway.

Together, she and Bobul managed to form a passable crib from chocolate, with some coconut straw to cradle the baby.

"Do you suppose she actually wants us to write Happy Birthday Jesus on this?" Becky asked, a bag of royal purple icing in hand.

"Hold on, I better check that little detail." Sam picked up the intercom and posed the question to Jen. "Looks like that's affirmative," she said a minute later.

"Whatever the customer wants, right?" Becky smothered a laugh and steadied her hands before starting the script.

Sam carried the cake out to the customer. "Here we go. It just wasn't quite finished yet. Thank you for waiting."

The woman seemed pleased enough with the free pastry and coffee she'd gotten, and she promised to come back. Sam watched her drive away and wondered which bakery now had a spare cake sitting in their store, waiting for their eccentric customer to come pick it up.

Kelly raised an eyebrow as Sam headed back to the kitchen.

"Whatever the customer wants," Sam reminded, although she had a hard time hiding a grin. She stepped up to the work table to finish the second party cake, a fairly standard sheetcake which Becky had prepped. Sam finished the company logo and a Happy Holidays greeting, and when the customer arrived a half hour later she was delighted with it.

By the time she got home that night, Sam had completely forgotten that she'd planned to find a safe hiding place for the odd magic box. It sat on her dresser, completely unaware that it had become the subject of such controversy and greedy desire. She looked around the room, trying to think what to do with it. Clearly, her attempt to do away with it permanently had failed.

She stared again at the box. *Strange little thing.*

One of the red stones winked in the lamplight. Did the box have some nearly-human affinity for her, Sam wondered. Had it come back to her house on its own or, more likely, had Sam dreamed that whole event? It was almost like a stray pet that had latched onto her. She reached out and patted the lid and swore the colors deepened as she did so.

Okay, you. We have to find a hiding place.

If, by some remote chance, Bunny Fitzhugh figured out that Sam possessed it, where would she be least likely to look? Sam put the jewelry into a drawer and cradled the box in her arm as she walked through the house. Bedrooms and desk were out—those would be the obvious places. She ended up wrapping it in an old towel and stashing it in the vent leading from the evaporative cooler. She wouldn't even consider turning on the air conditioning for months to come. She tightened the screws holding the vent cover in place and surveyed her work. It was high on the living room wall and well hidden.

"Now stay there!" she ordered as she brushed dust from her hands.

"Mom? Were you talking to me?"

Sam jumped, dropping her screwdriver.

Kelly closed the kitchen door as she stepped inside. A breath of chill air followed her.

"No, just fixing something. I didn't know you were home."

"I brought Chinese takeout. Sound good?"

Anything I don't have to plan, prepare, cook or clean up sounds good right now, Sam thought, taking a deep whiff of the fragrant containers.

She barely remembered eating the meal or falling into bed. Her dreams became a muddle of scenes from the Montague house, the bakery, and the lingering memory of Bunny Fitzhugh's piercing glare, her hunger for possession of the box. Except that in the dream, she wasn't called Bunny. She was Lorena.

* * *

Wednesday and Thursday passed in a blur. In one of their scanty conversations, Beau told Sam that he was wrapping up the loose ends in the Montague case, that it appeared the man was back in business and handling his consignments of art as usual. Life at the bakery became a whirl—customers with last-minute orders, dozens and dozens of pastries and cookies going out the door.

Thursday was designated as pie day. Sam, Becky and Kelly baked dozens of pumpkin, pecan, apple and cherry plus a few specialties like a chocolate peppermint crunch pie, more of the nutty-buttery fruitcakes and some eggnog cheesecakes. By the end of the day Sam felt as if she had piecrust permanently embedded under her nails and the scent of pumpkin pie spice wafting out of her hair. But the town was supplied with holiday desserts and her cash register was singing.

Friday was to be the final push. With Christmas Eve falling on Saturday, she planned to be open only a half day, with a little party for the crew and friends that afternoon, and then everyone could enjoy their Christmas Day at home.

Sam awoke Friday morning with her head full of plans but by the time she'd dressed, her kitchen phone began an insistent ringing. Delbert Crow started talking before Sam fully figured out who it was. He was emailing some kind of final release form that she would need to take over to William Montague and get signed. He wanted it in the mail today. Fine, whatever. She went to her desk in the corner of the living room, located the message and printed the attached form.

She drove her van to the bakery and spent an hour getting the early-morning routine going. Kelly and Jen quickly made the coffee and started serving up breakfast pastries, sending bags of them with office workers who were making the most of their final day of the work week. Boxes containing pre-ordered pies and fruitcakes stood in stacks on the back counter, awaiting pickup.

Sam stood at the front windows, sipping at her first cup of coffee and enjoying the sights of evergreen boughs on the shops and red bows on window fronts. She bagged a couple of filled croissants for each of her neighbors, along with a small printed invitation to the store party the following afternoon.

"We'll have a special cake for the event, and then I plan to box up everything that's left in the displays and take them to the homeless shelter," she told Riki, the dog groomer.

"Might I come along?" she asked in her charming British accent.

"Absolutely. The more the merrier, and maybe we can spread a little cheer."

Ivan Petrenko, the bookseller to the north of Sam's place, was equally enthusiastic. "I even can be including some books for the children," he offered.

Sam returned to the shop with a warm sense of Christmas spirit. It lasted up to the moment Delbert Crow called again. She promised to drop everything and get out to the Montague place right this minute, and she would drop the form in the mail at the Ranchos branch of the post office. Sheesh, the man was all business, all the time, she thought as she wished him a merry Christmas. She addressed an envelope and put a stamp on it, left the girls with instructions for the next few projects, then headed out to her van.

This time she approached the front door of the Montague place, ringing the bell and waiting what felt like a very long time before she spotted the flicker of a shadow at the peephole. She gave a little wave and said, "It's me. Sam."

Will stepped to one side of the open doorway and tugged Sam inside by her sleeve, quickly closing the door behind her.

"I see that you're still lying low," she said. "Sorry to bother you but my supervisor wants this final release form signed and mailed today." She held up the page.

"Sure. Come on in the study." He was wearing sweatpants and a plain t-shirt with a robe over it all, complimented by house slippers.

A laptop computer hummed on his desk, and folders littered the surface.

"I would have called first but I didn't have a number for you."

"Wouldn't matter. I'm not answering phones and I'm spending minimal time online right now." He sat in the tall desk chair, scanning the clutter in front of him.

This guy really is convinced that Bunny and her people know all and see all, Sam thought.

"The good news is that I've had a couple of sales. People buy big at the holidays." He patted the thick mat of papers, searching for a pen. The grip of a pistol showed as a sheaf of pages fell to the floor.

He noticed Sam noticing.

"I can't be too careful," he said simply. He found a pen and dashed his signature across the blank line at the bottom of Sam's form, without even reading it. She countersigned and had him repeat the process with the duplicate copy.

"This one is yours," she told him, folding the other

and sliding it into the prepared envelope. "And I guess that means we're done, as far as the USDA—"

Montague's eyes were riveted on something beyond Sam's shoulder. She spun around and came face to face with Bunny Fitzhugh.

Chapter 29

The woman's eyes blazed.

"Where is my treasure?" she murmured with a sibilant undertone.

Sam edged away from Bunny, unfortunately, also away from the room's only exit.

"William, I want that box. I know the old woman gave it away. You have it and I want it."

Bunny reached into the oversized bag whose strap crossed her chest. If she'd pulled out a magic wand and sent Montague flying across the room, Sam would not have been surprised. Bunny's short orange hair seemed electrified, standing out in spikes. Everything about her—the hair, the voice, even her clothing—seemed charged with power.

What she actually pulled out of the bag, however, was a

little more real—and a lot more frightening.

The black pistol looked huge in Bunny's small hand, but she didn't seem at all uncomfortable with it. She held it in front of her in a two-handed grip, demanding that Montague pay attention, daring him not to.

"Bunny, just slow down," he said.

Sam was amazed that his words came out clearly and calmly. As for herself, she felt about ready to wet her pants.

"I've got some paperwork right here," he said. "Just let me . . ."

He ran his palm over the surface of the papers on the desk then, so quickly that Sam didn't see it happen, grabbed up his own pistol, aimed it right at Bunny's heart, and fired.

Sam's ears rang and she dimly registered that Bunny folded like a puppet whose strings had been cut. There was blood. The black pistol slid a short distance on the oriental rug.

Bunny's arm twitched toward it and Sam backed farther away. Her shoulder bumped the edge of the bookcase, which she'd not noticed was standing open a tiny bit. Without thinking, she yanked the bookcase-door open and ducked inside.

A second shot sounded and Sam felt a tiny whimper escape her.

She looked up to find herself face to face with the ugly green Nazi robe. Her vision blurred and she grabbed for the inside handle on the door.

"Ms Sweet—it's okay. You can come out." Montague's voice sounded pretty shaky.

Bunny lay on the carpet with a widening circle of blood under her body. Sam took an unsteady breath and raised her eyes to the ceiling.

"I had to be sure," Will said. "Couldn't take the chance of her having any strength left to come after me with."

Sam lowered her gaze, but only to the level of the desk. Montague was unplugging wires from his computer and gathering his paperwork.

"What are you doing?" she asked. "The sheriff isn't going to want anything in this room moved."

"Honey, that is not my immediate concern."

"You're not going to report this?"

"I don't need to. I know you will. That's fine. But I won't be here when they come."

"Will, you have to be. You have to tell them it was self defense. She pulled her gun first."

"Yes, she did. And you'll tell them that."

"But you're a witness. You can't leave."

"*You're* the witness. I'm the killer. I'm not staying." He grabbed up the stack of files and the computer, hugging them to his body, and headed out the door.

"But—" Sam discovered that she'd dropped her pack near the bookcase. She picked it up and scrabbled with shaking hands to unzip the compartment with her phone in it. She pressed the speed dial for Beau's number and waited while at least an hour passed for each of the three rings before he picked up.

"B-b-b-eau, there's a—"

"Sam? What on earth is wrong, darlin'?"

"Wait." She forced herself to breathe in and out three times. While she did that she walked out to the hall, where she could hear sounds of motion from the master bedroom. "There's been a killing at Montague's house."

"He's dead? Oh, god, he was right about being in danger."

"Well, yes and no." She outlined the basics, and could hear him flip on his siren when she got to the part about Will refusing to stay and answer questions.

"I'm five minutes away. Get out of that house," he said. Before he clicked off the call, she heard him call radio dispatch and start rattling off code numbers.

She stood in the hall, wondering in a daze which door to head for, when Montague appeared at his bedroom door. He'd shed the bathrobe and donned several layers of warm clothing. A large backpack appeared to be stuffed to the gills. He slung it over one shoulder.

"Your sheriff buddy can call me if he wants. But I'm not sitting around here waiting for more trouble. Bunny was the main one, but Lissano's goons may still try for me. I don't know how much Bunny told Tiffany, but I'm not waiting around to find out."

With that, he ducked back into the bedroom and she heard the French door open and close a few seconds later. By the time she'd made it to the door, she only caught sight of a tiny flicker of his coat disappearing into the trees. She gripped her cell phone in her hand and let out a huge pent-up breath.

Three very long minutes passed before she heard Beau's siren. By the time he screeched to a stop in front of the house, her breathing had almost calmed down. Just a little.

She let Beau in the front door. "He's gone," she said.

He pulled her against his solid chest and she was content to simply lean there for awhile. But finally, Beau had to let her go and start doing his job.

Sam waited in the hall while he stepped into the study and checked the body. When he came back she told him every millisecond of the confrontation and shooting, in exacting detail. She had to close her eyes for a lot of it.

"Oh, baby, how awful for you," he said, pulling her close once again. He gave her a few minutes before he stepped back. "I hate to do this, but you'll need to repeat that whole story again, down at the station."

"I know. I figured as much."

"Right now, I need to radio my deputies and get them out looking for Montague."

"It won't do any good, Beau. He managed to stay hidden for three months the last time. He's good at it. And this time he packed clothes and probably some cash and some food. I don't know . . . it just doesn't seem very hopeful."

He lowered the hand that had reached toward his shoulder mike. "You're right."

"He isn't a murderer, Beau. It was self defense. I know I'll end up having to say that in court, but the story won't change. She drew on him first. If you'd seen her— She was wild."

He nodded. "Okay. I'll need to get her taken to the morgue." He keyed the mike and went into police code again.

Sam wandered to the kitchen, found a clean glass and filled it.. She felt tempted to start opening cabinets and break into the booze. But the day was young.

"My guess is that Montague will stay away long enough to be sure the law isn't after him, then he'll come back home," Beau said, coming to look for her once he'd summoned the medical investigator and ambulance.

Sam wasn't so sure, given Will's fear of Larry Lissano

and his belief that others were still after him. But she didn't say it. Anything could happen.

Chapter 30

There were so many loose ends. Sam felt like she was in the way as the medical investigator bustled in and Beau began the process that included trying to reach Robert Montague, locate next of kin for Bunny, and figure out how all the pieces of the complicated puzzle fit together. She finally asked if she could leave, knowing that getting back to business as usual wouldn't be easy. Her mind felt like a jumble of horrific images and sounds and thoughts.

"You okay?" Beau asked as she said goodbye at the door. "I could get the doc in there to give you something."

"I can drive," she said. "And I really can't afford to go home and collapse. I'll go to your office and give my statement and after that I'll be fine if I just get back to work."

But she wasn't fine at work, and when Kelly caught her weeping over a bowl of ganache that didn't turn out quite right, she drew the line and insisted that Sam go home. She found a bottle of Xanax in the medicine cabinet that she didn't remember—it must have been there for years, but she took one and slept for the rest of the afternoon.

When Kelly came home a little after six, Sam was sitting at the table in her robe and slippers, trying to coax herself into taking a shower and figuring out what to make for dinner.

"Okay, Mom, something happened and it must have been something awful. You do *not* fall apart at work." Kelly plopped a decently plump bank bag on the table in front of Sam.

Sam took a deep breath and outlined the basics, leaving out the real reason Bunny Fitzhugh had threatened Montague—the box. No sense it letting Kelly know her mother possessed an item that it seemed some really mean people wanted to get their hands on. She would either pressure Sam to get rid of it—which would entail revealing that she'd already tried—or, worse, might innocently let it slip to someone else that the box was in their home.

Kelly reached out and touched Sam's hand when she'd finished telling the story. "Feel like eating?"

"Something light, maybe. I can't seem to get motivated for much."

"You're not used to that Xanax," Kelly teased, opening a can of soup and putting the pan on the stove to heat.

I'm not used to any of this, Sam thought. She went into her bedroom and put on sweats and fuzzy socks. They set up trays in the living room and ate their soup to a background of some raucous game show. Sam felt her heart lightening a little by the time Beau called around eight.

"Sorry I didn't call earlier," he began. "We moved Mama to the rehab facility today, and by the time I'd finished at Montague's house and then got her taken care of, there was a ton of paperwork . . . Thanks, by the way, for giving Joe your statement already."

"I wouldn't have known it if you did call," Sam said, explaining how she'd come home from the bakery and fallen right into bed. "Anything new on Will's whereabouts?"

"Not a thing. The guy is good at disappearing. We've got a full-scale investigation going on Bunny, her connections to Global Imports, and whether it truly was Larry Lissano's men who made the first attempt on Montague's life. So far, it looks like Lissano himself isn't involved. He's been in Dallas all along. Global Imports has a small office in Albuquerque with, guess who, Tiffany Wright as the office manager. The company incorporated in New Mexico because it's so easy and cheap to form a corporation here, but their real operations are elsewhere."

"But you'd told me that Bunny's name was associated with the company?"

"She was added as a board member when she and Larry were still married. But she never had an active role in his business. He probably just forgot to take her name off the records when they divorced."

"But the two big men who got into Montague's house— they actually work for Lissano?"

"They do. We haven't been able to question them yet, but we have Tiffany Wright in custody. She's the one who said Bunny sometimes hired some of Larry's men for little extra-curricular jobs."

"You have Tiffany here in Taos?"

"Bernalillo County Sheriff's Department picked her up in Albuquerque for the breaking and entering at Montague's and transported her to us. We'd issued that warrant well before today's events. It seems that Bunny talked Tiffany into going to Will's house with her. Tiffany says Bunny wanted some kind of collectible box and told her that if Tiffany could get Will's art consignment records and destroy them, there would be no way the owners of all that art could prove anything. The two women would take everything of value and split it, then sell it on the shady-gray market."

"It's amazing how candid she's being about all this," Sam said.

"Yeah, well, she didn't start out that way. She thought she could bluff her way through until Bunny could come by with a lawyer for her. When she found out Bunny was dead, she broke down and started talking. Of course the spin is that everything Tiffany did was Bunny's idea."

"Naturally."

"It's probably close to the truth. I don't get the impression that Tiffany is smart enough to have thought of this all on her own."

"She may surprise you," Sam said. "She was certainly insistent on getting into Will's house the day I talked to her at the motel. Her whole focus was on getting that art and she's a pretty convincing little actress. But, like you said, without Bunny as the mastermind, she may just quietly slink away."

"Let's hope. My department can only question her for so long, then we have to let her go unless Will Montague wants to press charges on the B&E."

And they both knew how hopeless that was. The art dealer only wanted to stay out of sight.

Sam went to sleep with that thought on her mind and it bothered her half the night. If she could just convince Montague that Bunny was no longer a threat and that Tiffany deserved punishment for her own involvement. Even a short jail term might convince the younger woman that a life of crime was a stupid choice.

She woke and made her usual pre-dawn trek to Sweet's Sweets, where she found Bobul waiting in the alley, patient as an oak tree. He said good morning and without further comment went right to his work. He'd begun creating fantasy Christmas trees—dark and milk chocolate boughs with tiny garlands of finely spun sugar and intricate ornaments in white chocolate tinted a variety of shades. The work was amazing and Sam had put an even more amazing price tag on them, but the customers still snapped them up as quickly as he could turn them out.

Even though Sam had made no comment about the wooden box or the fate of Bunny—was she truly a new Lorena, come searching for what she'd believed to be hers?—Bobul seemed to regard her differently since yesterday. As if he somehow knew that the fate of the box, for now, was resolved. She watched him out of the corner of her eye and caught him doing the same a couple of times.

It wasn't long before the girls began to arrive for work and Bobul simply blended into the background, working steadily and quietly at his trees.

Sam gave a little pep talk about with this being Christmas Eve, everyone should convey positive attitudes and a joyful spirit to their customers. They wouldn't be baking a lot today, except to finish the cake for the wedding that was their last big order of the year, and get it delivered to the reception ballroom by two o'clock. The layers had been baked and stacked the previous day, so she set Becky to work making flowers.

"I have a little errand to run this morning," she said. "When I get back I'll finish the piping on this baby and we'll get her delivered."

She wasn't sure what she was thinking as she drove toward Talpa. The odds of Will Montague having come back to his home during the night or early morning hours were slim. But she couldn't let go of the feeling that she needed to talk to him one more time, that she might relay some of the information she'd learned from Beau last night and that the art dealer might be able to come back to the community he loved and take up his place once again. Knowing that her friend Rupert would probably come to her little bakeshop soiree this afternoon was another reason— maybe the real one. Sam wanted a positive conclusion to the art connoisseur's fate. She spent the better part of the drive sending out optimistic mental vibes on the subject.

There were no outward signs of life at the large adobe house, although she hadn't expected to see any. Montague was pretty adamant about staying out of sight. Still, it would be a lot more comfortable for him to hide out here than camping in the snowy woods or bunking in cheap, cash-only motels with thin walls and doors that gapped with cold air rushing in around the edges. She worked out this logic as she approached the front door and rapped sharply on it.

No sound whatsoever. Her taps even seemed to echo back hollowly. She gave it two more tries and then walked around to the back. The drapes were still drawn over the French doors to the living room, the way he'd left them yesterday. At the master bedroom doors, one drape was pulled halfway back, as she remembered it being in Will's flight toward the forested land behind. She rapped at the glass before pressing her face close to see past the reflected outdoor glare.

Clothes lay strewn on the bed. A couple of dresser drawers stood open, Will's hasty packing job still in evidence. It didn't appear that he'd come home.

Then she noticed something else out of place. Above the king-sized bed there'd been a painting by Peña. She remembered because Rupert claimed it was an original and fairly valuable. It was gone.

Her eyes darted about, taking in the other walls and the slice of hallway she could see from this angle. At least two other items were missing. She fiddled with her key ring, trying to remember if she'd given Will both keys to the new lock she'd installed. No. Sure enough, one of them was still on her ring. She dashed to the door to Will's living room and unlocked it.

The room itself was neat enough. But every piece of art—the paintings and the sculptures—were gone.

Chapter 31

S am walked slowly through the rooms, verifying, not quite believing. But it was true. The million-dollar art collection was missing. In the study, the bookcase door was securely closed. When she located the hidden catch in the desk drawer and activated it, she found that the hidden room still contained its cache of odd memorabilia. If Will took the art and planned to leave permanently, he surely would have taken this little trove as well.

Tiffany.

Sam knew she was in town, but Beau had said last night that she would be held for questioning as long as possible. It didn't seem likely that she'd had time to get out here and completely clear out the place. Sam tapped her foot, thinking.

Whoever took the art . . . how did they get it out? Will's vehicles. She hurried through the house to the connected garage. The Escalade, that large SUV, was gone. It wouldn't have been the safest way to transport valuable art, but she supposed if the thief weren't concerned about scratched frames and such, he or she might have managed to get it all into the cargo compartment with the seats folded down.

She studied the dusty garage floor, but too many people had been out here, including Beau at one point. There were plenty of footprints, but most were too blurred to be of value. What was she thinking, anyway? She hadn't the faintest clue how to recognize one footprint over another. She pulled out her phone and called Beau.

He promised to get out to the house as soon as possible, but it had been a morning busy with calls. There had been a rash of auto break-ins in shopping center parking lots, someone's idea of a cheap way to do their Christmas shopping. And he had to deal with the usual share of holiday drunk drivers and traffic incidents. At her inquiry whether Tiffany was still in custody, he said that she'd been released at eight o'clock this morning and given a bus ticket to Albuquerque.

That ruled out the main suspect other than Will Montague himself, Sam thought. No way Tiffany could have loaded up the Escalade and gotten away in under an hour. And if Montague had been the one to take his own vehicle and the art that was legally in his care, well, then there'd really not been a crime.

"So, should I stick around until you can get here?" she asked.

"No point in it. Lock up and I'll stop by the bakery for

the key. But I have no idea when that will be." He sounded tired, and he was only two hours into his shift.

Sam retraced her steps through the house, checking every window and door along the way. In the front hall, something shiny caught her eye. A metal button. She picked it up. It seemed familiar somehow, but she couldn't figure out how. She did know that Will Montague wasn't wearing anything with shiny metal buttons on it when he ran out the back door yesterday. She stuck the button in her pocket and finished locking up.

The showroom of Sweet's Sweets bustled with customers two-deep at the counter. Kelly and Jen boxed orders and rang up sales about as fast as they could. In the back, Becky held up a tray of holly sprigs and berries she'd made for the half-done wedding cake.

Sam hung her coat, washed her hands and picked up a large bag of buttercream frosting. Perfect strands of white flowed from the tip as she centered all her concentration on making them even. She piped strings, lace, and flounces on the traditional cake and was ready to place the greenery around the tiers when Beau walked in.

"Beautiful," he said, staring at the cake. "Maybe someday . . ." He let the thought drift away.

"How long have I been at this?" she asked, turning her neck to work out the kinks.

He raised his wrist and glanced at his digital watch. "I don't know. But it's nearly eleven-thirty now."

She stepped back from the cake to assess her work. The intense concentration had paid off—her rows were neat and straight.

"How's the mob out front?"

Becky spoke up. "Less mob-like. But the pies are gone and we're down to less than half the cookies."

"That's not bad. We'll close as close to twelve as we can, whenever there's a break in the traffic. I saved three pies back, for the homeless shelter. We can box up the cookies and whatever muffins and things are left."

Beau shuffled a little.

"Oh, right. I need to give you the key." Sam wiped her hands and went to the coat rack. She showed him the metal button she'd found and described where it was lying.

"I have a little something to show you, too." He glanced around. "Must have left it in the cruiser. Walk me out."

She followed to the spot where he'd parked in front of Riki's dog grooming shop. He reached in and brought out a newspaper.

Front page, the headline read: Shooting Likely Self Defense

Sam scanned the first few lines. "Sheriff's Department investigation and the statement of an eyewitness . . . will probably lead to a ruling of self-defense after a home invasion, say department spokesperson . . ." She looked up at Beau. "Thanks for not giving my name."

He shrugged. "Standard protocol."

"So, is this the final, official version?"

"Not quite. Mainly, I wanted to feed the story out there big and bold in hopes of getting Montague to realize he's not likely to face charges."

"Not likely?"

"That's all I can say at this time, Sam. He's going to have to answer questions. And they won't be easy ones."

She nodded. It was the best Will could hope for right

now. With luck, maybe Beau could keep references to him vague as well. *Local businessman*, or something like that.

"Well, I better get out there and write up a report about the missing art. That could end up being the bigger story, once the owners find out their stuff is gone."

"If you can make it by here this afternoon . . . once we clean up and deliver some goodies to the homeless shelter we're having a little party here. Cake and cider, coffee, things like that."

"Is it okay if I don't absolutely promise? There's just no way to know how the rest of the day will go." He reached out and tucked a forefinger under her chin, raising her face. "But I will definitely try." He kissed her lightly.

Kelly helped Sam with the wedding cake delivery— luckily, a smooth one. The bride would love it, her mother assured them.

When they got back to the bakery, Jen was in the process of helping two ladies who'd tapped at the door after the Closed sign went up. For the homeless, she'd already boxed half a cheesecake, most of the cookies, and a boxful of festively decorated cupcakes. Kelly helped her load them into the van, along with two bags of books Ivan had sent over, while Sam and the rest of the crew pitched in to clean up the kitchen. Bobul dried the bowls that Becky washed, and Sam put things away while running a mental inventory through her head, finally giving up and starting a written list of new ingredients she would need to order the following week.

"Who's up for the ride to the shelter?" Sam asked once the kitchen was clean to her liking.

All the girls chimed in, and Sam remembered that Riki

from next door had wanted to come along. They piled into the van with boxes and bags on their laps. Jen and Kelly wore the velveteen Santa hats they'd sported all week in the bakery. The lady who ran the shelter had tears in her eyes as she accepted the cheerful pastries and everyone's good wishes. By the time they got back to the bakery everyone was definitely in the holiday spirit, and Kelly couldn't wait to start the cider.

Ivan drifted over from his shop, bringing along the last two customers of his Christmas Eve day. Several other regular customers wandered in and out and Sam allowed herself to completely relax. Jen loved playing hostess and it felt good to let her take over, seeing that everyone had a slice of the square cake decorated as a present, in the shop's logo colors.

At one point Sam realized someone was missing and she walked into the kitchen looking for Bobul. Although not exactly a warm and fuzzy kind of guy, the chocolatier had made a huge difference to her holiday business. She'd planned a little extra cash bonus for him. But the kitchen was empty, with a hollow non-workday feel to it. Bobul's bulky brown coat and the cloth bag he always carried—the vessel for whatever mystical ingredients he brought with him—were all gone. Even the chocolate molds, which he usually left near the worktable in readiness for the next day's work, they were missing too.

She glanced at her desk and spotted a small brown object. The chocolate confection was a small box, an even closer replica to the real one than the one he'd given her his first day of work. She picked it up and held it on the flat palm of her hand. The quilted high points were dusted with a golden sheen, and in the grooves were small sugar dots of red, green and blue.

He knew who owned the magic box. He'd known all along.

It hit her that he wasn't coming back.

Chapter 32

Voices from the front room caught Sam's attention and she set the chocolate box back on her desk. One of the voices was Beau's. She walked into the sales room to find that several more people had come by. Zoë and Darryl were there—she in a shimmering broomstick skirt and a homemade sweater the color of a Caribbean turquoise sea, and Darryl with his white beard and hair neatly trimmed. Even though he wore jeans with his red western shirt, a couple of children stared at him with the question in their eyes—Santa?

Rupert was here, chatting with Ivan the bookstore owner who didn't have a clue that he was speaking with the real Victoria DeVane, bestselling romance novelist. It was a well-kept secret within the book world and Sam knew she was one of the prolific writer's few confidants.

But the person her eyes sought out—Beau—managed to stay low-key, even though he still wore his uniform. *Sheriff Cardwell*, she thought, *you are by far the best looking man in the room. Okay, in the town.*

He looked up just then and his smile widened. It sounded old-fashioned, Sam knew, but her heart really did flutter a little when they connected like that. He excused himself to the man he'd been talking to and edged through the gathering toward Sam.

"Hi darlin'," he said. "You are a welcome sight."

He was too, truth be told, even though both of them were still in their work clothes. His hair was a little mussed, as if he'd just pulled off his Stetson before he came indoors. She hadn't actually looked at herself in a mirror all day and had the sudden urge to smooth her own hair down, just in case.

"What do you mean, a welcome sight? Rough afternoon?"

"It's been a very full day, for sure." He ran his nails down the side of his face, as if checking to see how much his beard had grown since morning. "I haven't told you the latest."

Sam cocked her head, waiting.

"We got an anonymous tip about that missing art. Phone number was a pay phone in San Diego."

Hmm?

"The caller gave us the address of a self-storage place near Questa. Said to check unit 73. I explained the value of the missing paintings to the judge, got a quick warrant, and went out there with two deputies. I think it's all there."

Sam felt her jaw drop. San Diego meant Robert Montague. "But who put the art——? How did Rob know——?" The gold button. An image of Rob putting on his camel jacket flashed in her mind.

Beau shrugged. "I do know that with the missing pieces in hand and those consignment records that we took from Montague's place earlier, we have a good chance of getting all the stuff back to the rightful owners."

"What about the missing vehicle? Any sign of that?"

"Nothing. We've got a 'be on the lookout' for it, but who knows what that might turn up."

"I just don't get it," Sam said. "Will Montague had a good business here. Why would he do this? Give up everything and hit the road?"

"I don't know, darlin'. The man may have a lot more problems than we know about. Maybe he'll eventually see a newspaper or learn that he's in the clear on the murder charge and he'll come back."

She noticed a tiny smudge of chocolate on her palm, from the miniature box Bobul had left for her. When she raised her hand to lick it off, the answer came to her. Will Montague must have contacted his brother and told him to take the art. They'd met up at the storage unit and stashed everything.

"Maybe Montague will get over his fear of Larry Lissano and his men, or whatever besides Bunny sent him into hiding?"

"I have to check the statutes," Beau said. "There's got to be a period of time, thirty days or sixty days maybe, where I can hold the art in hopes that he comes back and claims it. But after that I'll have to contact the owners and return it to them. We can't tie up their property forever."

Sam puzzled over the mysterious Montague, still not figuring out his motives. Beau touched her arm.

"Anyway," he said, "it's not your problem any more. Relax and enjoy your guests."

"You're right. We don't always understand what makes people do weird things." Or collect weird things. She pushed the vision of the cluttered hidden room aside and smiled at Beau.

"You never exactly told me what you wanted for Christmas," she said. "So you're getting a surprise."

He sent her the slightly lopsided smile that always melted her heart. "I may just have a little surprise for you too. You and Kelly are still coming out to the house in the morning?"

One of the customers stepped up and started talking, but Sam gave Beau the nod about their Christmas plans. He whispered that he needed to get going. Sam turned her attention to the lady, who was raving about the chocolates she'd bought a week earlier.

"I don't know how you made those, but they changed my life! I've had more energy this week than I've had in years and my—"

The words faded as Sam thought of Bobul and the changes he'd brought to her shop. She decided to stop by the cabin in the canyon later and try to talk him into coming back.

"—just wanted to let you know that I hope you keep carrying those candies." The woman gave Sam's arm a little squeeze and walked away.

Darkness was settling by the time their little gathering wound down. Sam cleared cups and neatened the showroom before turning out the lights. Kelly had a party to attend with friends, so Sam walked alone out to her van.

Thick snowflakes had begun to fall, leaving a half-inch of white on everything. Sam turned on her wipers and decided to take the long way home. She cruised the near-empty streets leading to the plaza and pulled into the quiet square. Electric luminarias crowned the tops of the buildings, most of which were softly lit with holiday trim, all of it blurred by the snow in the air. The old-fashioned street lamps cast pools of golden light on deserted benches. It was Currier and Ives with a New Mexico twist. She parked beside the La Fonda Hotel for a few minutes, letting the peaceful scene soothe her soul.

"Thanks, I needed that," she said aloud as she pulled away from the curb.

Highway 64, winding through Taos Canyon was equally quiet. The snow was still slushy and her tires had no trouble finding traction. She followed the curves until she came to the spot where Bobul had directed her to turn when she brought him home that night. Her headlights hit the rustic logs.

The cabin was dark. She sat in the van with the engine off, listening for any sound, her window open to any whiff of woodsmoke. Nothing. She got out and walked up to the front porch.

The steps were broken, one missing entirely. It hadn't been this way a week ago. When she looked up she saw that the front door was missing entirely, the window beside it broken out. Her headlights sent a sliver of illumination through the openings. There was no comfortable recliner, no bed, no firewood.

"Bobul?" she called out. "Are you here?" The man who

had shown up like a gift from the universe, at the exact moment she needed him, was gone. A heavy feeling settled in her heart.

She called out one more time, knowing it was futile. Her voice merely echoed back at her. No one had lived in this place in years.

Chapter 33

Sam half expected to wake up in the morning to learn that it was only December first and that the past three weeks had never happened. The sight of Bobul's uninhabited dwelling made her previous visit there feel like some strange figment of her imagination. Yet she knew it wasn't. The chocolate box he'd left sat on her kitchen table, right where she'd placed it when she got home last night.

Kelly's bedroom door was closed and since they weren't due at Beau's house until ten, Sam walked around the house in her socks, letting her daughter catch up on her sleep. She brewed coffee and drank a cup of it, black and strong.

By the time Sam had showered and decided on which blouse would be right for the occasion, she began to hear Kelly stirring. They shared a wide slice of coffee cake that

Sam had brought home as day-old two days ago. It had held up surprisingly well, but Sam knew she would be ready for the waffle brunch Beau had promised, followed by a full Christmas dinner sometime in the late afternoon.

"At least the roads aren't bad," Kelly said as they donned their coats. "It stopped snowing around nine last night, I think."

The drive to Beau's ranch property north of town was beautiful. The sun had risen in an absolutely clear sky, giving the deep blue that most parts of the country couldn't even fathom in winter. It sparkled off the fresh snow as if a billion diamonds had been flung to the ground. Sam steered her truck through the tall log pillars that marked the entry to Beau's property, the twenty acres with pasture, horses and barn. The large log home looked solidly nested among the low snowdrifts.

Beau greeted them at the door, wiping his hands on a dishtowel. "Ready for the finest waffles and bacon you've ever tasted?" he said with a grin. He stepped aside so Kelly could enter first, then he stepped forward and slipped his arm around Sam's waist.

"Merry Christmas, darlin'." He gave her a long kiss.

From inside the house came a shriek.

Sam looked up to see Kelly racing across the room to where Iris's wheelchair sat in a square of sunlight from the bank of south-facing windows. Kelly threw her arms around Iris.

"I've missed you so much!"

Sam almost swore she called Beau's mother grandma. She walked in and gave Iris a hug, too. "It's so good to see you back at home," she said.

The old woman's eyes sparkled with moisture. "It's good to be home, too. Even if it's just for a day."

Her speech was still a little blurry, but better than the last time Sam had seen her.

She noticed for the first time that Beau had cut a fresh tree from the property and set it up in a corner. Blue spruce, over eight feet tall. Small red lights were woven through the branches and ornaments that looked like they came from the 1940s added bright touches of color.

"Mama's favorites," he said, noticing the way Sam was examining them.

"That's nice."

"So, everybody—waffles first or presents first?" he asked.

The smell of bacon from the kitchen had already caught Sam's attention. Everyone voted for breakfast first.

As they ate, Sam noticed that there were a few nicely wrapped gifts under the tree and she began to fret. There had been absolutely no spare time for shopping, and her main plan to give Beau and Iris season tickets to the theater in Santa Fe had been squashed when she got the news of Iris's stroke. She'd ended up finding a feather-soft bed jacket for Iris, something she should be able to use even after her recovery, since she was wheelchair bound anyway.

Beau had been a harder giftee. They'd become very close but she still was a little uncertain where the relationship was going. Beau had fallen harder and faster than she, but she was getting used to the idea of a committed relationship. She hoped her gift wouldn't be taken the wrong way—it was at once frivolous and serious.

There was something about watching an older person at

Christmas that reminded Sam so much of Kelly's childhood holidays. Perhaps we really do come full circle. Iris truly delighted in each gift. She raved every bit as much over the bed jacket as she did later over the box of chocolates Kelly brought and then the books and wristwatch that Beau gave her.

When it came time for Sam to hand over her gift to Beau, she waited until Kelly and Iris were sitting together across the room, Kelly reading the opening chapter aloud from one of Iris's new books. Sam reached into her pack and drew out the slender rectangular box.

Beau took it and gave a little shake. "A watch? The box is the right shape."

She shook her head, having severe qualms.

"Well, I better just tear into it," he said. He ripped off the paper, opened the lid of the box and stared. "A toothbrush." He picked it up. "A pink toothbrush." Turning it over, "In fact I'd guess that it's a used, pink toothbrush."

Sam felt about fifteen again. "It means that I hope you might be willing to put this in your bathroom and have me stay over sometimes."

He set the package on the nearby coffee table and took both her hands in his. "Darlin', I'm willing to have you stay over always."

She blushed. They were face to face kneeling in front of the tree, their knees almost touching. "It's not awkward? I mean, would Iris be okay with it?"

"I mean, Samantha, that I would be honored to have you stay over, always and forever, permanently."

Her heart stopped. "Oh, my gosh, Beau, is this a proposal?"

He nodded. "I think it is. I mean, I know that's what I want. I just didn't quite get around to picking out a ring and getting flowers and really doing this right." Now it was his turn to look flustered. "Oh, man, I'm really messing this up."

She reached for his hand again, the one he'd raised to his forehead. "You're not messing anything up, Beau. It's a downright beautiful, totally surprising proposal."

"That's not quite a 'yes.' See, I knew I was messing it up."

"It's a yes," she said.

Chapter 34

The reality of the proposal didn't quite hit Sam until she got home that evening. Amid the shrieks from Kelly and the smiles from Iris and the toasts with eggnog and the turkey dinner that they prepared together in Beau's kitchen, Sam let herself be carried away with the dreamlike quality of the day.

They talked about when, where and what the wedding might be.

"Valentine's Day," Kelly said. "It's the absolutely most romantic day of the year."

Sam couldn't remember a whole lot of romantic Valentine celebrations in her own life. She'd never actually come close to being married and there were only a few half-serious relationships in her past. She'd conceived Kelly in the heat of a quickie while working in an Alaskan pipeline camp and never even told the father that a child existed. She'd spent her youth being a mom and working her tail off to support her daughter. The men she'd dated were good for movies, dinners, the occasional sex at their place while Kelly and a babysitter waited for her to come home. Beau was truly the first man she'd become emotionally close to.

"We'll talk about all that later," he'd said. "I think Sam is maybe a little bitty bit overwhelmed. This whole month has been a tough one."

He had that right.

The conversation trailed off to other areas as dinner wound down. Sam and Kelly were clearing plates when the phone rang. Beau took the call and came into the kitchen with a solemn expression.

"William Montague's SUV was found. It went off I-40 near Gallup. He was alone and didn't make it."

"Was it the storm?" Sam asked.

"No, the highway was clear and dry. The snow we got here stayed north of the interstate."

Sam stared at the open dishwasher with its racks of cranberry encrusted plates. How sad.

"There's a little more," Beau said. "State Police said there were skid marks and broken glass on the roadway. Not from Montague's vehicle. They think someone may have run him off. They knew just where to do it too, a place where the dropoff is real steep."

Sam swallowed hard. Someone had killed him; she knew it. Bobul was right about there being dark forces out there. Will Montague was out of the picture. Bunny was dead. Tiffany was still out there. Bunny might have told her all about the wooden box and now Tiffany could come after it. Or Lissano's goons. Sam got a sudden image of the two hulking men following Will out to that dangerous stretch of road.

All of this ran through her mind as she drove home from Beau's house. Kelly had offered to stay overnight with Iris, but Beau said he was under orders to get his mother back to the rehab facility by nine p.m. They'd come on home while he took Iris back.

Now, with Kelly asleep in her own room, Sam realized that there were some crucial things to be addressed before she could marry Beau. Things he didn't know about her.

She found her screwdriver, went into the quiet living room and took the air conditioner vent cover off. The towel encasing the wooden box was a little dusty but the box was reassuringly sound. She pulled it out, replaced the metal louvered cover, and carried the box to her room. She sat cross-legged on her bed with the bundle on her lap.

She couldn't imagine keeping the secret of the box from him. She'd told him very little so far, and always managed to explain away her sudden bursts of energy, her odd powers of observation. But he didn't have a clue as to the depths of the box's magic or any knowledge of its history. And she wasn't yet sure she could tell him.

Solid, country boys just didn't go in for this sort of woo-woo stuff. She imagined telling him the stories of Lorena and witches, and the visit to Bobul's sad little cabin that really wasn't even livable. If he didn't immediately have her committed, he certainly would think twice about wanting to marry her. Her heart ached at the thought of hurting him.

But how could she *not* tell him? Keeping secrets was a sure way to ruin a relationship. She'd tried to get rid of the box and the responsibility of it, and that didn't work. She stared at the lumpy little thing in her lap.

Cold and abandoned for several days, the box was dark and gloomy when she unwrapped the towel. She looked at it. *You won't ever be beautiful, will you?* she thought. As if reading her thoughts, the box began to warm in her hands. Soon the carved wood began to glow with a golden hue and the stones radiated color.

Okay, I guess you've proved me wrong more than once. I don't know why this fell to me, but I guess I'm meant to keep you, to safeguard your secrets and try to use your powers for good purposes. I would say that I'm supposed to take care of you, but I have a feeling it's just the opposite. You are going to take care of me.

Sam let go of the box and sat up straight. What on earth was she doing talking to a box? Okay, she hadn't spoken out loud—had she? But she was having a conversation. She looked up to be sure Kelly hadn't gotten up and that she wasn't observing.

Sam was alone.

Now that she'd heard the legends about the box and witnessed the lengths some might take to attain it for themselves, Sam knew that she had to be careful. She had to protect herself, and her loved ones. It went beyond simply not appearing to her friends like a nutcase. There were powerful forces out there in the world, and people who would do anything to gain that power.

This harmless-looking little chunk of wood had been given into her care. Like it or not, Sam knew this was somehow part of her destiny. She went to her dresser and began to neatly sort her jewelry and place it inside.

More stories with Samantha and Friends!

Samantha Sweet breaks into houses for a living.
But she's really a baker with a magical touch,
who invites you to her delightful pastry shop
—Sweet's Sweets.

Don't miss the next fun book in this series!

Sweet Hearts
Will it be Valentine wedding bells for Sam and Beau?
Samantha's pastry shop, Sweet's Sweets, is busier than
ever this Valentine week, as Sam struggles to replicate
the magical chocolate-making techniques of her prized
chocolatier, the man who boosted her winter holiday
sales into the stratosphere.

However, candy classes take second place to a new
mystery, when Sam meets a woman whose missing son's
case seems to have been dropped by the authorities.
Marla Fresques learns that she is dying and needs for her
son to come home and raise the daughter he left behind.
Sam agrees to help, hoping that Sheriff Beau's inside
connections will bring about a quick and happy resolu-
tion. But what about Sam and Beau's wedding plans?
They may be in jeopardy when an entirely new develop-
ment appears in the form of one of Beau's former lovers.

Connie Shelton is the bestselling author of the Charlie Parker mystery series and the Samantha Sweet mysteries. She has taught writing courses and workshops and is the creator of the Novel In A Weekend™ writing course, available online at www.novelinaweekend.com She and her husband live in northern New Mexico.

Sign up for Connie's free email mystery newsletter at
www.connieshelton.com

Contact by email: connie@connieshelton.com

Follow Connie on Facebook and Twitter

CPSIA information can be obtained
at www.ICGtesting.com
Printed in the USA
LVOW10s2213300417
532790LV00008B/732/P